STAG AND HOUND

Geonn Cannon

Supposed Crimes LLC • Matthews, North Carolina

www.supposedcrimes.com

This book is typeset in Goudy Old Style, licensed by Ascender Corporation.

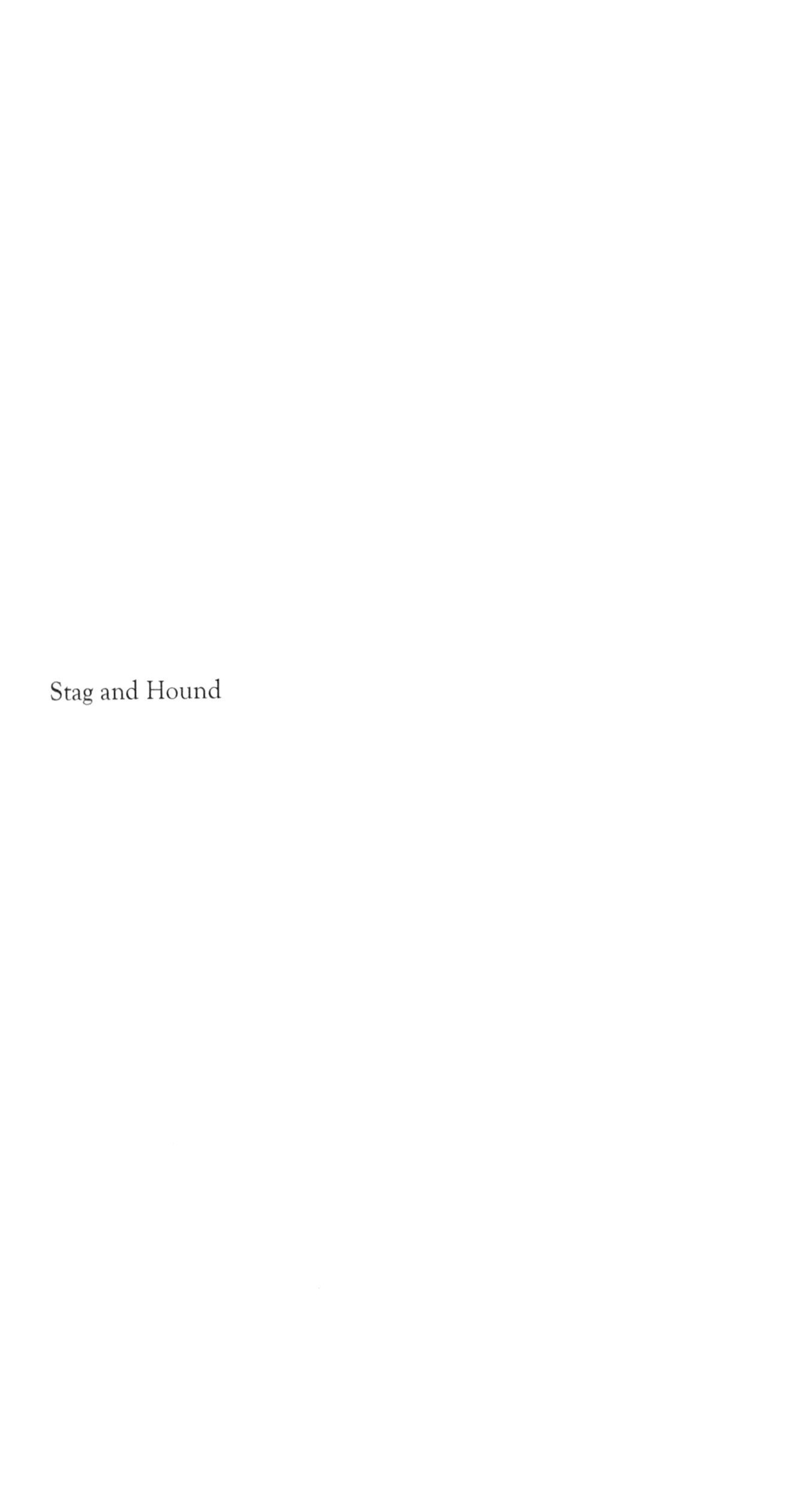

Stag and Hound

PROLOGUE

THE TWO German officers spotted the first wolf just before dusk.

It was easy to get spooked at this post. The train station felt like the sole remnant of a long-dead civilization, forgotten as nature reclaimed the area. The shadows stretched out over the slow setting of the sun and darkness drew over the station like a shroud. Now the space between the platform and the trees seemed like a solid wall of black.

The ranking officer was Franz Richter, and his subordinate was a shaky new recruit named Oskar Arndt. Their shift began when the sun was still out, so the dreadfulness of the place only became clear after it was too late to back out. Richter liked the cold and the darkness. It gave him time to think and contemplate other postings that would be better suited to his temperament. He could be a guard. He could watch over the prisoners and ensure they stayed in line. He craved that kind of responsibility, and taking mediocre assignments like guarding a desolate depot was just one of the steps necessary to achieve that height.

Richter thought about the wolf he'd spotted just before the sun went down. He had pointed it out to Arndt, aiming with two fingers until the younger man saw the flash of gray-and-white piebald fur moving through the trees. Richter had brought up his rifle to track the beast, but he didn't fire. Even if the trees hadn't been in the way, they were trying to keep a low profile. They didn't want to frighten people in the neighboring village by randomly shooting off their guns at whatever wildlife happened to wander past. Besides, he happened to like wolves. They were majestic creatures. He wondered if the wolf was out there now, watching them. He considered putting out some of his rations to see if he could draw it into the light.

Neither officer admitted to being frightened, but both men had gripped their weapons just a little tighter as the last of the light fled. They remained at their post, standing on the platform next to the train depot. Two lanterns had been hung ten feet apart, one on each side of the small shack they were ordered to guard. The men stood at the point where the two penumbras of light met to form an oval-shaped oasis of brightness.

It was almost midnight before they heard the second wolf. Richter moved forward and clicked his tongue, then whistled loud to frighten the beast off. Arndt watched the older man move forward, but his attention was drawn away by the sound of something on the tracks. The scuttle of claws on gravel indicated it was just another wolf, but he was jumpy and on edge. He swallowed the lump in his throat and flashed his torch in the direction of the noise, hoping the animal would be frightened away.

Instead the dirty yellow beam illuminated a wolf with either white or yellow fur, its eyes reflecting the light back to him in an eerie and unnatural way.

"Go," Arndt said. "*Husch.*"

Something clattered behind him, bouncing off the wood so loudly and suddenly that Arndt spun toward it. He dropped the flashlight in order to hold his gun with both hands. His palms were so slick with sweat that he feared he would drop the weapon. The platform behind him was empty. He hissed Richter's name, assuming the older officer had simply moved out of the light, but he received no response. He looked over his shoulder at the wolf on the tracks. His fallen flashlight cut through the darkness and made the wolf's shadow fall long and slender over the rails.

The object he'd heard fall was resting on the edge of the

platform. At first he thought it was a branch with an oddly gnarled end, but when he knelt down and shone his light at it he recognized it as a severed arm in a sleeve. He recoiled away from the gruesome discovery, a shout of alarm dying in his throat even as the piebald wolf they'd seen earlier leapt from the shadows. Its teeth were bared as it flew at him, and he barely had time to get his weapon up before the beast was on him.

Simon like the streets of Monthyon, the little commune in the north of France they had chosen for their base of operations. The houses were small castles made of gingerbread, their windows and doors cut out of the otherwise blank faces. The narrow streets wound aimlessly around each other, forming strange arcs and turns that would make pursuit difficult for anyone unfamiliar with the layout. Simon panted as he ran down the curving road. The blood of the fight still spotted his fur, but no one seeing it would question blood on a wild animal.

He and Sandrine had shed their wolf skins just long enough to set up their plan. They moved quickly to complete their mission, all too aware of the two dead Germans growing cold on the platform above them. When their relief arrived at dawn they would find the corpses and begin looking for signs of sabotage. They would find nothing, and the deaths would be written off as animal attacks. He, Sandrine, and other members of their pack had spent the past week letting themselves be seen to create a history of wolf sightings in the area. The next train would roll in on schedule, and the tracks would buckle where Sandrine had sabotaged them.

Simon didn't know how many casualties to expect. He didn't want to know, but he knew Philip had it calculated to a close approximation to what the actual death toll would be. There would be too many innocent people at the station or aboard the train, civilians just doing their job or complying with their occupiers out of fear of standing up for themselves. Simon didn't let himself worry about the collateral damage, but Philip couldn't bring himself to ignore it.

The important loss would be the depot itself. Until it was repaired, the Germans wouldn't be able to use it to bring in more weapons or men to this area. They couldn't call the mission a success until the train actually crashed, but he was confident they would have reason to celebrate come mid-morning.

They rounded a sharp corner to a tangle of streets that broke off into alleyways and dead-ends, the perfect place to lose any potential pursuers, and vaulted over a pair of iron gates preventing vehicular traffic from passing through. Their hideout was a two-story chalet on a tiny spur of a street, easy enough to overlook under the best of circumstances but currently further obscured by a Peugeot parked in front of five trash cans and a wheelbarrow. Simon slipped easily between the blind and the stucco wall, and a few seconds later Sandrine followed.

A side door had been left open just enough for Simon to nudge it with his snout, and he pushed into the dark workshop on the other side. The room reeked of oil, grease, and sweat; the product of their past few weeks of work. They stopped long enough to transform once they were inside, rising onto their hind legs as their wolf sides melted away to be replaced with sweat-beaded flesh. Simon pushed a wave of black hair out of his face as he entered the home.

Sandrine turned left, toward the private rooms on the upper level. Simon went to the right and pushed open the door to Philip's den. The other man was sitting on the divan with his back to the door, head bowed in slumber or to read. Simon walked across the room to the minibar and glanced over as he came around the couch. Philip had a book open in his lap, but looked up when Simon came into view.

Simon's body was lean and corded with muscle from long nights running across the French countryside, his transformations helping burn off any excess fat. He felt Philip's admiring gaze on him as he poured himself a drink. He feigned indifference as he poured, but his body betrayed his arousal at being stared at. He felt himself stiffening as he brought the snifter to his lips and took a drink, ignoring his erection as he turned to face the leader of their cell.

"I assume this means the mission was a success," Philip said.

Simon walked to the divan and stood in front of the other man. Philip's shirt was undone at the throat to reveal a hint of his collarbone and the hairless chest underneath, and Simon idly used the forefinger of his free hand to tease the heavy cotton out of the way. Philip put aside his book and moved to perch on the edge of the cushion. He spread his legs and Simon stood between them. His cock twitched as if it could sense Philip's proximity, and Simon moved his hand from the shirt to Philip's thick blonde hair. Philip moved his head with the caress.

"Tell me what happened."

"Sandrine performed admirably. We took the guards by surprise and sabotaged the tracks. By noon we should know for certain if it was successful."

Philip nodded and brushed the back of his hand up the inside of Simon's thigh. His balls tightened from the touch and his cock grew harder until Philip could turn his head and brush his lips over the shaft. Simon grunted and closed his eyes, brought the glass up to his lips, and took a small sip as Philip kissed his way to the head. He explored with a multitude of soft kisses, teasing the foreskin with his tongue before reaching up to push it back with a ring of his thumb and forefinger. Simon planted his feet on the carpet and moved his hand to Philip's shoulder, stroking the curve of his neck.

Their first time had been in the wild, just after escaping from a trio of German troops. They tore off their clothes and transformed into wolves as they fled, crashing through the underbrush and tumbling through the tall grass and clover in a pell-mell race to safety. They only relaxed when they had crossed a river, dropping to the mud on the other side and spinning to make sure the coast was clear. They transformed again and fell back on the ground, laughing with the giddiness of their close call.

Simon's eyes had been closed, his hands on his stomach, when he felt Philip's hand on his hip. His laughter trailed off but his smile remained as he reached down and moved the other man's hand to the root of his shaft. Philip's fingers had obediently wrapped around him and began stroking the length, twisting his hand around the head before traveling back down. Simon's breath had gotten quicker and he lifted his hips to meet Philip's strokes.

It didn't take much work before he grunted and spilled onto Philip's fingers. He'd caught his breath before he opened his eyes and looked at Philip. Neither of them spoke as Simon rolled over onto his elbows and knees. He could hear Philip's ragged breathing as he positioned himself, and Simon gripped the ground with both hands as he pushed inside. There was nothing romantic about that first coupling, nothing more than a pair of wolves fucking on the banks of a river.

But in the past two years it had become something more. Simon looked down as Philip closed his lips around the head of his cock. He brushed the blonde bangs back so he could see his lover's face. Philip looked up and then took Simon deeper, his hand now cupping Simon's balls and stroking them.

Simon squared his shoulders and lifted his head. He saw that he'd left the door open. Sandrine was standing with one arm against the doorframe, the light from the room illuminating her body and the lower section of her face. She was biting her bottom lip, one hand stroking her breast through the lightweight shirt she'd put on after changing forms. The other hand was captured tightly between her thighs. The cut of the shirt was high enough to see the curve of her bare hip.

The light reflected off her eyes, and he smiled before closing his. She'd watched before, and there was no harm in letting her enjoy the sight. Philip had moved beyond teasing and was now working only toward orgasm. He moved his free hand to his pants, eagerly working at the buttons to free his cock as well. Once he had it in his hand he stroked quickly, pulling back to swirl his tongue over the head of Simon's cock, pursing his lips to give it resistance as he pushed back down, moaning and curling his tongue along the underside of it.

Simon looked past the divan to Sandrine. She had moved her hand into her shirt, her knuckles making mountain ranges against the fabric as she pinched her nipple. Simon moved his hips faster and Philip grunted in response. He let go of Simon's balls and slid higher, moving between the cheeks of his ass to push inside with his thin middle finger. Simon arched his back and came before he could stop himself, throbbing against Philip's tongue only a heartbeat before his come filled his lover's mouth. He rolled his head back on his shoulders and bit the inside of his cheek to keep from howling his release.

He pulled his sensitive and softening tool from Philip's mouth, its purpose met, and dropped to his knees as Philip sank back on the couch. Simon didn't tease or explore, he simply batted Philip's hand away and took the erection into his mouth. The skin was smooth and warm to the touch, so it didn't take much before Philip came as well. Simon swallowed what he could, letting some of it spill out onto the pale purple head of Philip's cock just so he could gather it up again with liberal use of his tongue. Philip grunted and his body jerked with each touch, his fingers tangling Simon's hair in post-orgasmic bliss.

"Do you think we should adjourn to bed?" Philip asked. "We likely won't know anything until late in the day tomorrow."

"Bed sounds ideal." Simon kissed the head of Philip's cock again before tucking it away, buttoning the fly again before standing up. He glanced at the doorway and saw that Sandrine had already vanished, most likely returning to her room to finish what she'd started. Simon took Philip's hand, leaving the den's lights on and the forgotten book on the couch. They didn't have to be awake until at least noon the next day, and he had a great many ideas for how they could earn a lie-in.

After Simon's orgasm Sandrine retreated to the stairs. She moved quickly on the balls of her feet so she wouldn't make too much noise. She knew Simon had seen her, but she didn't want to distract the men too much from their evening. The image of Simon's body was stuck in her mind, the perfect line of muscles from his chest to his abs as if the muscles were forming an arrow to his cock. Nudity was hardly taboo in the pack; they couldn't be prudish about their bodies if they were going to be transforming in front of one another. But in her mind Simon's body was different, worthy of adulation and the occasional furtive peek.

When she got to her room, a cramped nook at the apex of the house, she stripped off her shirt and reached between her legs again. She rested her other hand on the bedpost and closed her eyes. She didn't want either Simon or Philip in the way they might have thought. She wanted to be one of them, wanted to feel the other man's lips around her cock until she could spill into his mouth. She bit her bottom lip and furrowed her brow as she rubbed the heel of her hand against herself. She didn't want Philip inside of her. She wanted him bent over the side of her bed with his cock in his hand while she fucked him as hard as she wanted.

Philip's room was adjacent to hers, and she opened her eyes when she heard the door click shut. His bed had one leg that was shorter than the others, and it thudded quietly against the carpet as the mattress took his weight. The sound was followed by a second thud, and then a third and fourth. She moved her hand in time to the rhythm they had set. She moved her hand off the bedpost and mimed stroking herself as her other hand stroked between her legs.

She could hear Philip moaning through the wall and she added that to her fantasy. She came before either of them did, biting back her cry of release and arching her back as if she could ejaculate over the sheets. Spent, she turned and dropped onto the mattress, her legs apart and her chest rising and falling with each breath as she stared at the ceiling.

On the other side of the wall, the steady thud of the bed's short leg continued. It was occasionally punctuated by a grunt or a sigh, a growled direction followed by a body adjusting heavily on the mattress. Sandrine looked down past her breasts and the flat of her stomach and used her hands to mold the shape of a cock over her dark pubic hair.

In the middle of stroking her imaginary erection, a new sound added itself to the sounds of fucking from next door. Not the sharp breath of her pack mates or the familiar thud of the shortened leg against the floor. It was a furtive brush of shoe leather against slate tile. Sandrine immediately ceased her masturbatory fantasy and sat up, eyes on the water damage in the corner of her room. The sound came again, longer this time, and she could almost see the shape of a man sliding down the roof to brace his foot against the gutter.

She was on her feet in seconds. She banged her hand against the wall to alert Simon and Philip before she stooped to pull on her boots. She didn't bother with any other clothing, but she did sling a belt around her waist so the sheath bumped against her naked thigh as she ran. Outside her room was a ladder to access the roof. She was already undoing the latch when Philip came out of his room. She looked back and saw him tying his pants closed, the shape of his cock pressing against the thin material.

"Intruders," she said. An instant later she was on the roof.

The wind caught her black hair, whipping it around her face

and compromising her vision for a very vital half-second. When she could see again she barely had time to react to the fist swinging toward her face. She pulled her knife free and drew its blade across the man's fingers. His blood fell in warm droplets her arm. She shoved him backward and he tumbled from the roof. He and the first man had come from next door, having ascended the trellis in the backyard. She knew that no one would attack from the roof unless...

"There are men at the door!"

She didn't wait to find out if Simon and Philip heard or acknowledged her warning. The man who had slid down to the gutter was there still. Sandrine bared her teeth and lunged at him as he brought one arm up. Flame seemed to spark from his hand, and a second later she heard the gunshot echoing off the neighboring buildings. The bullet tore a sizeable chunk from her upper arm, but it did nothing to slow her momentum. She slammed into the shooter and wrapped her arms around his thick chest, carrying him with her off the edge of the roof.

Sandrine used the man as a landing pad, the bones in his upper chest and neck cracking as they met the pavement. She released his clothes and spun to face the house. Their windows were shuttered but she could see the light of gunfire within. Something crashed against the wall and she heard a howl of pain. Two men who had been hunkered in the alley were rushing her. Sandrine picked up the dead soldier's weapon and fired once, taking out the man in the lead. She grabbed his uniform jacket and used him as a human shield as she rushed the other one. He sank three bullets into his compatriot's back before Sandrine threw the dead body aside and grabbed the second soldier's head. She threw her weight to the side and snapped his neck with a fluid, balletic motion.

She dropped him to the pavement with his friends, then dropped to sniff them. She had caught a whiff of something, but her brain was so tuned into the fight that she wasn't able to identify it. Now that the men had been dispatched she could focus and...

Her eyes widened as she recognized the smell. "Bomb."

She was through the door in one leap. Two people were fighting in the living room, but only one was mostly naked. The smell of his sweat and flesh marked him as undeniably Simon, even though she could still strongly smell Philip all over him. She clapped her hand down on his shoulder. He dispatched the man he was fighting and spun on Sandrine, lifting his hand to strike her before he recognized her by shape and scent.

"Bomb," she said.

"Philip is in the den."

They only had time to start toward the hallway before that entire side of the house shuddered in response to a blinding flash of light. The concussive wave from the explosion cracked the walls, funneling down the hallway to create a fist that punched Sandrine and Simon in their chests. They were thrown back against the front wall of the house as a wave of fire followed the initial blast. The place they had called home for the past year was suddenly engulfed with flame. She didn't realize she had lost consciousness until Simon jarred her back to alertness by dragging her to the door.

She pulled away from him, coughing as she rolled onto her hands and knees. She transformed as quickly as she could, aching in the small of her back where she'd impacted the wall as she limped through the smoke and ash. Simon had transformed as well, and she grabbed the leg of his pants with her teeth to help pull them off. They stood together and watched as flames spread across the face of the house. Something on the second floor collapsed, and the resulting flare pushed out the shutters on every downstairs window.

Sandrine was lightheaded from losing consciousness, but she knew they couldn't stand around watching their house burn. The chalet had been compromised, and they had no idea how many more enemies were waiting to descend on them. She threw her weight against Simon's side. He whimpered but didn't look away from the house. Sandrine was twitchy with anxiety as she hunkered down and looked up and down the street. She half-expected to see uniformed officers coming down every alleyway, peeling out of the woodwork with weapons in hand.

Simon lifted his head and howled in frustration and sorrow. Sandrine knew the back yard's fences were too high for a wolf to leap. Even if Philip had gone out that way he would have been trapped by the heat and flame. There was nothing they could do for him now. They could only protect themselves from being caught in the same trap. She looked at Simon and knew he was only thinking about Philip, so she ducked her head and bit down hard on his left foreleg. He yelped and danced away from her. She snapped her jaws at him and moved away from the fire.

Simon looked from her to the ruins of the chalet, which now seemed alive with threat and danger. The shutters swung in the hellish breeze from within as if the house was breathing. Simon chirped again low in his throat and turned away from the house. Sandrine turned and began to run. He could keep up with her or not, it was his decision. She'd done her part and now she had to ensure that at least one of them got away. She ran through the streets of Monthyon, the routes she had taken so many times in anticipation of a moment just like this. Every movement she caught in the corner of her eye was a threat, and every pair of headlights was an enemy transport.

There were other members of their cell elsewhere in Monthyon. Their priority now was to ensure everyone else was safe, then they would relocate to a secondary location that their enemies hopefully didn't know about. She understood that Simon was mourning, and Philip's death was a horrible blow to them all, but the simple truth was that if they got out of the night with only one casualty it would be a bloody miracle.

CHAPTER ONE

Six Months Later

IF MONTHYON had been a maze, Paris was the mythological labyrinth. Narrow streets surrounded on all sides by buildings so tall a visitor couldn't get their bearings, switchbacks and turnarounds that forced cars into circuitous paths, and roads that appeared to be dead-ended until closer inspection revealed a one-lane brick path leading away from it. The tangled grid of alleys and byways had proven to be godsends for the remnants of their cell; the wolves quickly learned the ins and outs of their neighborhood so they could escape if they needed to. Simon knew the route to safety backwards, forwards, and sideways, and he still couldn't draw a map of it even if he wanted to.

The alcohol may have been partially responsible for that. He was in an illicit pub, the name of which he'd never bothered to note, staring at an empty glass. He didn't remember ordering or drinking it, but he could envision the bartender filling it multiple times. It was a sight he could bear to see again, so he rapped his knuckle on the bar and motioned for another round. He would be awake and alert for his pack, to keep them safe if need be, but he would numb himself as much as possible for those damnable conscious hours.

He was grateful for Sandrine. He was supposed to be the leader, the one coming up with the plans and making sure everyone stuck to them. But he just couldn't. Every time he tried, his mind told him to leave it to Philip. Then he remembered it all over again. They remained in Monthyon long enough for their plant in the fire brigade to confirm they found three bodies inside the house. Two of them were armed, but one was undeniably Philip. So Simon found himself frozen in grief.

Sandrine picked up the slack. She was the one who found places for them to hunker down and hide. She was the one who paid off the landladies and the police to look the other way. He knew how much she hated to talk, and he was forcing her to talk to everyone just to make sure their people were safe and protected. Just to cover his ass.

He picked up the glass which had been refilled as if by magic and brought it to his lips. When he put it down it was half empty. In the mirror behind the bar he could see Sandrine approaching him. He finished the drink and pushed the glass away as if he had been planning to leave even if he hadn't come to drag him back. As she settled on the stool next to him, he ran a palm over his face and felt the rough growth of his beard. He could also stand a trim; his hair hung loose and greasy over his sunken eyes. He was pale from staying indoors drinking all day. His hands trembled because he hadn't let the wolf out in over a month.

Sandrine folded her hands on the bar and said nothing. He refused to be the one to break their silence so he just stared directly ahead. She didn't have to scold him or point out that she was the one keeping the pack from devastation. She knew that he was well aware of how pathetic he was. The thought of what Philip would think if he could see the wretch his lover had become made him sick to the stomach. He grimaced as if Sandrine had said the words aloud and ran a palm over his face.

"I know," he said out loud.

She looked at him and then picked up his glass. She sniffed the residue, held it up to the bartender, and curled her finger so he would bring her one as well.

"Is everyone settled?"

She nodded.

"Didier?"

"Not happy," she said with a shrug, indicating that very little would have made the cantankerous old man happy. "Not complaining. Too loudly, anyway." She took a sip of her drink and made a face, spitting to one side as she nudged the glass away with the back of her hand.

Simon reached over and took it from her. No sense in good booze going to waste, especially in times like these. He emptied the glass and put it down to see Sandrine had slid a piece of paper over in front of him. He looked at the paper, looked at her, and picked it up. His fingertips, wet from holding the glass, left smudges behind as he opened it. The writing on the inside had been scrawled against a soft surface, so they resembled a child's drawing rather than actual words. But he squinted and managed to make out a time and a place with Thursday's date. At the bottom of the sheet were the words LT K Mackay.

"What is this?"

"Meeting."

"I can see that." He turned on his stool so he could face her, one elbow braced against the bar so he didn't fall over. "Who the hell am I meeting?"

Sandrine kept her eyes on the bartender to make sure he was too far away to hear her. "Brit."

Simon laughed. "He can hang. Who set this up? It wasn't you. You'd never go to the limeys for help. Not even in a shit storm like this one. Irene? Was she the one?"

"None of us. His people contacted us."

That was unexpected. "We're not charity. We don't need help." She stared at him until he looked away. "It's only been six months," he added.

"That's six years in wartime. We need help."

"We need Philip."

Sandrine held a steady gaze on him.

"We don't need an outsider coming in and telling us what to do. How to survive. We've been surviving just fine by ourselves. Besides, you're a fine leader. You got us to Paris. You found places for us to hide right under the Gestapo's nose. You will keep us safe."

"Go to the meeting."

"Or what, you'll quit?"

"Or I will cut you from the pack."

He flinched and looked at her. "You wouldn't dare."

She slid off her stool and walked toward the exit. Simon rose and pursued her outside.

Drifts of snow had accumulated against the side of the buildings and further reduced the passable space between them. He stopped and looked at blanket of white, wondering just how long he had been inside the tavern, but Sandrine kept walking. She had to lift her feet in a marching pace just to clear the crust of snow, and that gave him the chance to catch up with her. He grabbed her arm and forced her to look at him.

"You can't just cut me from the pack."

"You're cutting yourself out," she growled. "You sit here drinking all day, spending what little money we've managed to scrape together, mourning a man who would punch you in the face if he knew how you were wasting our time. The pack needs you. It does not need to drag dead weight, not at a time like this." She snatched the paper from him and held it in front of his face. "Either you go to the meeting or I will go in your stead. I will make it my first act as this pack's leader. My second act will be exiling you. Good luck surviving on your own, you pathetic sot."

She shoved the paper back into his palm, forcing his fingers closed around it.

"Tomorrow. Zero-nine-hundred. Either I will see you there or I will never see you again. Make your choice."

She turned her back on him and walked away. He watched her march until she turned a corner and left his sight. The speech had stunned him. Sandrine knew the value of her words, and he knew that she would never speak ten if two would suffice. She had just spent a fortune to dress him down. He respected that enough to sober up, if just a little.

He looked at the paper in his hand. He did not want some British interloper getting in their way. And Sandrine had just proven that she would be a leader worthy of succeeding Philip. But he also knew it was not a position she would have chosen for herself. He didn't want to trap her in it against her will. That could lead to sloppiness and death.

LT K Mackay. Simon folded the note and stuck it into his jacket pocket. He would be there in the morning, and he would bring this British stranger into the pack. It was what Philip would do in his place. That didn't mean he had to like it. At the very least the meeting would satisfy his curiosity about why the Brit wanted to meet. He would size Mackay up and ensure he was a good fit for the rest of the pack. If he was, Simon could relax and let him take over. If not... he could cross that bridge when it became necessary.

For a moment he considered going back into the tavern, but he knew how Sandrine would react if he came back drunk after her speech. His jacket and scarf were meager protection against the cold. He cinched it shut at the waist and fastened the buttons up to his throat before he trudged away. He would have a hangover, but that was unavoidable. He took a deep breath of frigid January air and focused on getting himself home without being stopped by anyone with a badge or a weapon.

Lieutenant Kenneth Mackay tried to ignore how flimsy the floor felt under his feet, just as he was ignoring the temperature of the night air that whipped across the exposed flesh of his face. He had to push those things far out of his mind so he could focus on the task at hand. Ordinarily he didn't have a problem putting aside discomfort for the greater good, but this time was different. He hated being in the air, and he didn't know any *canidae* who felt differently. It was hard enough getting over his instinctual aversion to flight, but the wolf side of him accepted it was a necessary part of the war. Now, though, he was asking the wolf to jump out of a perfectly serviceable airplane with only a backpack between him and certain death.

Intelligently, he knew the safety statistics of what he was about to do. He had been instructed in the proper procedures and was confident he would reach the ground safely. That did nothing to calm the primal fear and his racing pulse. He stretched out his fingers. He clenched his hands into fists. And he measured his breathing to ensure he remained calm until they were over the drop zone. The officer safely strapped to the plane's hull gave him the thumb's-up. Kenneth managed to copy the gesture, looked out into the endless dark, and took a running leap into oblivion.

He spread his arms and legs as soon as he was clear of the plane, hands slightly raised so they would be even with his face. He plummeted faster than he expected, blind to everything on the ground save for a few lights in the towns huddled around the outskirts of Paris. He knew in the daytime it would be a green, yellow, and brown jumble, an earthen stained glass surrounded by thick and mossy forest. It was winter now, and hopefully the ground would be covered with a nice cushioning layer of snow. He was aiming for one of those forests now. That was the plan, at least. He hoped the wind predictions and the flight plan were both accurate. If not, he was about to land in enemy territory with no idea where to go or how to find help. The only thing in his control was the ripcord, and he tugged it to release the parachute and end his freefall.

Kenneth landed without incident, exhaling sharply as he trotted a few steps across uneven farmland. He caught his breath and used a flashlight to check his compass. He could just barely hear the planes droning engine in the distance. They were going in the correct direction, it seemed. That was a good first sign. He turned his light to his wrist and checked the time. He had four hours to make his meeting, and he doubted the resistance cell would wait for him if he was late.

He quickly shed his pack and flight suit, gathering them both into a satchel that would slip over his forelegs. Once he was naked he dropped down into a runner's starting position. He let the transformation pass through him like a full-body shudder, his bones and muscles twisting and popping into a new arrangement. He resisted the urge to howl his joy at being back on the ground and settled for stretching his legs.

Sorry, old boy, he thought to his primal side. *Needs must when the devil drives. But now you get to really show off. The countryside is yours. Get me where I need to be and everything else is up to you.*

He felt the wolf taking over. It was a general wash of animalistic and mindless urges. The scent of the forest bloomed into life all around him. At the moment it didn't matter that this was enemy territory. The only thing that mattered to the wolf was that it was new, unexplored territory. It paused long enough to slip its front legs through the straps of the satchel. The bag was designed so that it could be tightened and secured by taking a strap in the wolf's jaws and pulling tight. Kenneth did so, jumped and darted in a quick back-and-forth motion to ensure it wouldn't move around too much, and then gave over the reins to the wolf.

The animal's extreme joy washed over him as it broke into a dead run. Four hours to the rendezvous point, and the wolf could move ten times faster than a man. Even better, a wolf wouldn't get stopped by German roadblocks or asked for its papers. That would give his four-legged alter ego ample time to explore the wonders of the Parisian forests before it was time to get to work.

CHAPTER TWO

SIMON'S FUR was mottled black and white, markings that gave him the appearance of having rolled through ink. He had traveled the ten kilometers to the rendezvous point by following the Seine, and now he hunkered under a low-hanging branch to wait for the British officer. Dawn was coming and Mackay was late. It didn't bode well for the man or the mission; if he'd been compromised there was a chance the entire pack was in danger. If he was simply late, then they would have to reconsider just how trustworthy the man would be in a life-or-death situation.

He couldn't wait forever for the man to show up. He was debating just how long he could remain at a potentially compromised position when a white-and-tan wolf trotted around the corner. He wasn't carrying a pack, but he scanned the area and changed direction when he spotted Simon. Simon stood up and could sense the intelligence behind the other animal's eyes. He huffed to show his irritation, and Kenneth snorted and shook his head. Simon huffed again, then turned and jogged away. Kenneth fell in behind him.

The two wolves remained close to the trees, dropping out of sight whenever they heard the rumble of engines. Traveling in wolf form was safer and faster than being bipedal, but there was also a chance some German troops would decide to have target practice with them just as a lark. They moved cautiously along the river until they were close enough for the streets to start looking familiar. Simon indicated for Kenneth to follow carefully and weaved through the maze to their safe house.

Didier was waiting by the front door smoking a cigarette. He watched them approach and swung the door open at the last moment, swinging it out of the way just before Simon crashed into it. He changed direction and went down a short corridor to a drawing room overstuffed with furniture and further darkened by blackout shades over the windows. Sandrine was sitting on the couch with two other members of the pack, all of whom turned to face the new arrivals.

Simon finished shifting in time to observe the final stages of Lieutenant Mackay's transformation. The man was a scarecrow; broad in the shoulders and narrow at the waist. He had definition in his chest and arms that proved he was no lightweight, his hands spreading out from thin wrists like the roots of a sapling tree. His face was narrow and weighted down by his jaw and slight overbite. When he pushed the sweat from his forehead into his hair, the pale brown strands stood up like a crown of thorns.

Sandrine brought the men some clothes. Simon stepped into his trousers and drew them up. "You were late. I almost left you behind."

"It was an unavoidable and unpredictable snag," Kenneth said as he pulled on his own pants. "I ran across a group of Gestapo in the woods. They saw my satchel and assumed I was being used as a carrier pigeon. I attempted to evade them but one of them was a hunter. It was either allow myself to be captured and my pack searched or risk having him shoot me. I lost my clothes and my supplies, but there was nothing to identify me. I finally managed to bite one on the hand badly enough that they let me go to tend to his wounds. I had to find my way to the rendezvous by dead reckoning. In the dark. In a country I'd never been in."

Simon said, "It doesn't matter if you have an excuse. All that matters is that you were late. If it happens again, we're leaving you."

"So noted."

"This is the group. That's Sandrine. Claudine and Ambrose

are over there. Didier was the man by the door. There are others, and you'll meet them as necessary."

Kenneth said, "Excellent. Wonderful to meet you all. I'm Lieutenant Kenneth~"

"Loupin," Claudine said. "We all share the same last name. It solidifies us as a pack, and it provides anonymity should any of us be captured."

"Ah. Very well. Kenneth Loupin, although Kenneth will suffice." He nodded his thanks to Sandrine for the clothes. "I was sent here for two reasons. One is because you lost your Alpha..."

Claudine said, "Philip was not our Alpha. He was simply our leader."

"Right. Secondly, I have information about the night you were attacked. You've been under the impression that your cell was specifically targeted. That is not true."

Simon frowned. "It felt pretty fucking personal."

"I'm sure it did," Kenneth said. "But you were just one of seven cells attacked that evening. British Intelligence believes it was a concerted effort to cripple the resistance in the north-central regions. Seven houses attacked. Thirteen dead." He gestured to a pad on the table and Ambrose handed it to him with a pencil. He quickly began filling the top page with writing. "I know that these cells are arranged so you know as little as possible about the other members. It's a safety feature that is unfortunately working against you this time. Everyone thought they were the sole targets so no one thought to look at the bigger picture."

Simon took the paper from him and saw he'd drawn a crude map of north-central France. Monthyon was marked with an X, along with six other cities forming a cluster in the same area.

"When you were attacked, you fled somewhere safer. You came south, to Paris. The survivors from the other attacks also fled... some to Paris, like you. Others to Sarcelles, Saint-Denis, or Villeroy. The retreat meant that the entire region was left empty of any resistance. We believe that what happened was simply a scare tactic to drive everyone away."

Sandrine said, "Why?"

Kenneth blinked at her in surprise. "You speak?" She stared at him, waiting for a response to her question. He cleared his throat and said, "Yes. Well, we're not sure. But the mere fact they went to such lengths just to create a diversion is worrisome. It means something is going to happen there and they don't want to risk sabotage. I have been tasked to take you back north to see what we can discover. If the Krauts are setting up something big, it will be up to us to make sure it never comes to fruition."

Simon put down the pad. "And that's why you're here."

"And that is why I am here, yes. Whatever they were trying to keep quiet, they've had a six month head start to get it under way. Time is of the essence, so I would like to leave as quickly as possible. I have a list of names, people in the area who are sympathetic to the resistance and may be able to provide information about what's been happening."

Didier said, "Have you been in battle before, son?"

"I was in Dunkirk in 1940."

Didier sneered. "An evacuation. What a feather in your cap..."

Kenneth squared his shoulders and stared Didier in the eye. "We held the Nazis back long enough to evacuate three hundred thousand people. We made them change course and abandon their attempts to invade Britain. Those troops are turning the tide of the war as we speak. Without them we would be outmanned and outgunned, and Britain would have no defense against invasion from Germany. We would be in the exact same situation France is, and I don't have to tell you what a disaster that would be. We needed our troops out of there, and we spent two weeks ducking artillery fire to make it happen. We lost good men on that beach, but we saved hundreds of thousands. You would do well to thank me for that, because those men are France's only hope at being free again."

"Dunkirk also showed us miracles are possible, even in a world as dark as this one." Everyone looked at Simon, surprised he would step up in support of the newcomer. He shrugged. "No one believed the evacuation would be successful, let alone result in so many lives saved. France surrendered to the Germans a week later. It was a good time to be reminded that the good guys could still win even though things looked grim."

Didier snorted again but didn't continue the argument.

Simon continued, "We can be ready to go by this afternoon.

We'll spread out and get in touch with the rest of the pack, let them know what the plan is. Didier, Sandrine, you take the truck. The rest of us will travel on foot so as not to attract attention." He looked at Kenneth. "While everyone else is packing up, I'll show you the route through town. I don't want to waste time looking for you if you take a wrong turn somewhere."

Kenneth said, "Thank you. Does anyone have a map?" Claudine produced one and unfolded it on the table. They gathered around as Kenneth drew a kidney-shaped circle over the countryside around Monthyon. "The center of the retreat seemed to be in this area, near the bend in the Marne. We don't know if that's significant, but it's the best information we have. So we'll set up here, in Isles-les-Meldeuses. That should put us close enough to find whatever is going on and hopefully put a stop to it. We'll leave as soon as everyone is ready to go."

Simon folded the map. "Do you need time to recover before transforming again?"

"Even if I did, we can't afford it. I want to learn the route as soon as possible."

"Fine." Simon turned to Sandrine. "Coordinate with Didier and make sure everyone knows the plan. I want everyone out of Paris and in Meldeuses by tomorrow morning."

Sandrine nodded and went to retrieve Didier from his post at the door. Simon began shedding the clothes he had just put on, glancing over as Kenneth did the same. The British officer was built similar to Philip, but he was more muscular in the upper body. Simon looked away and dropped to his hands and knees. He transformed and looked over to see the change take over Kenneth's body.

It was a beautiful sight to see a person become a wolf, to witness the shift between man and beast. Kenneth's face twisted and pulled against itself to accommodate a long and blunt snout. His fur exploded across his shoulders and shimmered down his back like a wave on the ocean. When the transformation was complete he lowered his head and shook himself, huffing noisily as he checked to make sure Simon was also in his wolf form. Simon gave a nod and Kenneth turned to lead the way out of the house. Sandrine held the door open for them and Kenneth stepped to one side.

Simon paused on the threshold, met Kenneth's gaze, and then took off into the frozen alleys of Paris.

It quickly became clear to Kenneth that Simon wasn't interested in taking it easy on him. The streets were riddled with cutoffs and turnarounds, dead-ends and blind corners. There were piles of dirty snow clinging to every building, some drifts as high as the windowsill. The bricks were either slushy or icy under his pads, depending on which street they were on and how much sun exposure it had. There were shop owners who would jab at the wolves with broom handles as they passed, which forced them to duck or skip to one side to avoid a blow to the head. Simon would occasionally slip or skid when he made a turn, but it was very clear that he knew these streets extremely well.

Kenneth struggled to stay on his feet and avoid the swinging broomsticks while keeping an eye out for Gestapo and trying to keep Simon in his sights. He was panting by the time they reached the main avenue. Sweat clung to his fur and his tongue lolled sloppily out of his mouth as he stopped to catch his breath. Parisians bundled against the cold would step aside and exclaim at the wolves in their midst, although they refused to call them such. It was always "wild dogs" and "blasted strays." What was undeniably a wolf in the forest became a dog in the city; it was the way people's minds worked.

They cut southeast onto Rue de Rohan and passed under a trio of archways into Carousel Square. The tight streets and meandering passages gave way to a sprawling open area spanning between the Arc de Triomphe du Carrousel the forecourt of the Louvre. Simon stopped on the grass and turned to face him, but Kenneth was too awed by the splendor of the place he suddenly found himself. It was the Paris he'd always imagined when people talked about the magnificence of the City of Lights. He could smell the Seine even over the crush of bodies and the stink of too many military vehicles.

People surrounded them, both civilians hurrying about their business or police and military officials. They couldn't linger, as people were already converging on the two apparent strays. Simon huffed and bounded to one side, jerking his head toward the arches leading out of the square. One of the German officers was fingering the leather strap of his holster as he wandered closer, and Kenneth knew that he was planning to get off a little target practice. It was definitely time for them to go.

He let Simon lead the way again, ignoring the shouts of German and Frenchmen alike as they ran away. Kenneth half-expected to hear a crack of gunfire, but it never came.

CHAPTER THREE

KENNETH LEANED against the wall of the mud room, stretching his legs out in front of him. He curled his toes and flexed his fingers in an attempt to get used to the new shape of his limbs. There was always a period of adjustment after a lengthy transformation. Quickly changing from wolf to human and back again had exacerbated the sensations this time, and his hands were pins and needles now. He was also sore and sweaty from pursuing Simon in a maddening chase through Paris. They'd traced main escape routes and backup paths. Kenneth hadn't set foot in Paris before that morning and now, barely past lunchtime, he felt as if he could draw a map of it from memory.

The walls were thin enough for him to hear the pack's voices in the other room. He knew they were going over the finer points of moving their entire operation back to the north, but they also had to be talking about him. He lingered in the darkness to give them all a chance to have their say. He was a professional interloper; this was the fourth time he had been sent to provide information and support to an established cell. He knew what to expect from them: mistrust, paranoia, aggression, and wariness. He was an unknown entity. They didn't know what he would be like in a pinch, and he couldn't prove his worth until the moment presented itself.

It was true in reverse as well. All he knew about the Loupin pack was what he'd read in their files. When the heat was on, he thought he knew which ones were trustworthy and which ones would be of the most use in certain situations. The pack, like every pack he had been temporarily assigned, knew and trusted each other implicitly. He was envious of that loyalty. He hadn't felt it since just after Dunkirk, when he and the last pack he was permanently assigned to were forced to disband.

The memory left a bad taste in his stomach, so he pushed it aside. The voices had died down, so he wasn't surprised when there was a knock on the door. Simon entered the mud room without waiting for a response. Kenneth made no attempt to cover himself even though he was still nude, and he caught Simon's gaze lingering ever so briefly before he handed over a folded outfit.

"You're in luck," he said. "You and Gilles are about the same size. You can wear these until we leave, and then you can pick up some more outfits when we arrive at Isles-les-Meldeuses."

"Aces. Thank you, Simon." He took the clothes. As Simon was about to leave, Kenneth added, "Today... was that about testing me or proving your superiority?"

Simon narrowed his eyes. "What are you talking about?"

"Putting me through my paces? Come on... the Louvre isn't on our escape route. You were just showing off. Were you trying to prove you're tougher than me or just seeing if I had what it took?"

"The life of every person in this pack relies on every other member pulling their weight. I wasn't playing games with you out there, Mackay. We've all worked together for years. We trust each other. You're an unknown quality. I don't like having someone I don't know on a mission like the one we're about to undertake."

"Don't know or don't trust?"

"It's the same thing, *n'est-ce pas?*" He glanced down again, this time making no attempt to hide the fact he was examining Kenneth's body. Kenneth made no attempt to hide. "Get dressed. There are other members of our pack here, and I want them to meet you before we all split up and head north again. I want them to see you and get your scent."

"I look forward to meeting them."

Simon grunted noncommittally and stepped out of the room,

closing the door behind him. Kenneth looked through the clothes - simple tweed pants and an olive wool shirt - and began dressing. He had worked with other packs before, and he knew that gaining their trust would be an uphill battle. Even non-*canidae* soldiers were slow to welcome in someone like him. The situation was even tougher this time due to the circumstances of his arrival. By all accounts Philip was a beloved leader. There was no trick to charming his new troop, no shortcut to being accepted. The only thing Kenneth could do was put his head down and prove his worth through actions.

He finished dressing and smoothed a hand over his hair. The soreness had faded from his body and he was once again human in both body and soul. He tugged on the pointed collar of his shirt and made a mental note to thank Gilles for his sacrifice when and if they ever met each other. He left the mud room and went to introduce himself to the rest of the Loupin pack.

The next hour was spent with Kenneth, Simon, and the fifteen members of the pack gathered around the map to devise their path out of the city. Simon didn't want too many of them traveling together, so he chose two routes and arranged a staggered departure time for each group. "We'll leave markers when we can. Dangers to watch out for, troop movements, that sort of thing. If we need to detour we'll have alternate routes here and here." He indicated them on the map.

Didier said, "We got to Paris just fine without all this nonsense. Why not just go back the same way?"

"We came down here in a mad dash," Simon said. "We got lucky. We have to be more cautious this time."

"Because of him?" Didier said, glaring at Kenneth.

"Because what he says makes sense. Because losing Philip was enough, and I'm not going to lose anyone else because we acted stupidly. If you have a problem with that..."

Didier grunted but didn't continue his argument. Simon finished explaining the routes and then split everyone up into groups. Sandrine and Didier would go in the truck first. They would be followed by two groups of three. Two more groups of three would follow an hour later. Simon and Kenneth would bring up the rear so they could clear out the safe house and make sure there was nothing that would reveal to their enemies where they had gone or who they were.

Before leaving town, Sandrine took the truck around to the other safe houses. The rest of the resistance members would take only what they could carry, and the truck would be loaded with any weapons, rations, clothing, and whatever else they didn't want to leave behind. She returned to the main house to pick up Didier and offered her hand to Simon through the window. He clasped it and pulled her almost halfway out the window to roughly clap her on the back.

"We'll see you up north. Be safe. Do not let Didier drive."

She grinned and settled back in her seat as Didier snorted at the insult.

"Watch your back as well," Didier said. "I don't trust that *rosbif*."

Simon stepped back from the truck and let her pull away from the house. As soon as the truck was out of sight, Simon gestured for everyone who remained to go back inside. "We'll eat before we go. Not all of us had lunch, and it will be a while before we're settled enough to have another meal."

Another pack member, a lifelong Parisian named Leopold, grabbed Simon's wrist as he passed. Simon gently removed the hand before he could say anything.

"I see it." He looked at Kenneth. "Inside. We may not have much, but you can have Sandrine's share since she's not here." Once they were inside, Simon closed the door and completely changed his demeanor. "How many?"

Leopold said, "Four at least. They're waiting for reinforcements."

"They don't know how many people we have in here. They're not willing to risk it." He looked at Kenneth. "There are men—"

"At either end of the street watching us from the second floor windows. Yes, I saw them. One man appeared to have a handie-talkie."

Simon appeared impressed. "Any suggestions?"

"We can't wait for their reinforcements to arrive. At the moment we definitely have them outnumbered. There are thirteen of us here. The question is whether we can approach them without drawing attention to ourselves."

Leopold said, "The true question is whether they have people following Sandrine and Didier."

Simon cursed under his breath. "All of our precautions will be useless if they do. Gilles, get on the radio and try to get in touch with Sandrine. Warn her."

Kenneth said, "You know this neighborhood better than they do. Is there an alley or a back way to get in there?"

"Yes. There is an alleyway that connects all the buildings on this side of the street. We could get someone into their buildings through those exits if they're unmanned."

Simon scanned the rest of the pack and a line appeared between his eyebrows. Kenneth could follow his train of thought: these men and women weren't battle-tested. They could pull off sneak attacks and guerilla tactics when necessary, but Simon was reluctant to send them into an open combat situation.

Kenneth stepped forward. "I'll take the building to the south."

"Good. Anatole will go with you." To Anatole, he said, "Stay a few paces back. Give Lieutenant Mackay room to work and watch your back. If he needs you, he'll let you know."

"Right." Anatole looked at Kenneth and nodded, shifting his allegiance from Simon to his new commanding officer.

Kenneth returned the nod. "Happy to have you at my back, sir. Shall we go as we are, with weapons, or will this require a more feral touch?"

"I'm keen on feral myself," Anatole said. "But you've been changing a lot today, so..."

"No such thing as too much. Feral is fine by me."

"Then lead on."

"The rest of you give us five minutes to get into position. Then begin making a spectacle of yourselves. Whatever you have to do to get their attention while keeping yourselves safe. Draw their eye. Make them think we're about to make a run for it."

Gilles said, "We'll keep 'em occupied. Give 'em hell, boys."

Simon chose Leopold as his backup. The four men moved through the house to an erstwhile servant's entrance that led into a cramped alley. They stripped down and left their clothes inside, transforming before they stepped outside. Simon and Leopold went north, while Kenneth led Anatole off to the south. He felt the thrill of charging into battle, the hairs on his forelegs and along the back of his neck standing up as he rounded the corner. The building that housed their enemies was straight ahead, and its back door was only guarded by a pair of metal garbage bins overflowing with refuse. Kenneth's heightened senses picked up the reek of decay from the food, but he forced himself to move past it.

The door could have been an obstacle to their attack. Kenneth planned to do a quick switch back and forth to use his hand if necessary, but he spotted an open window to one side. The ice made his leap tricky but his paws caught the sill and he pulled himself up and inside. He dropped to the floor, claws skittering against tile in what appeared at first glance to be a pantry. He stepped out of the way just as Anatole dropped in. He landed in a crouch, much more graceful than Kenneth's entrance had been. He squatted slightly to indicate he would remain in the pantry according to the plan, and Kenneth moved toward the door.

He could hear voices on the other side speaking quietly, but he could tell they weren't speaking French. He nudged the door open with his shoulder and slipped through into a dark kitchen. Again he was assaulted by the smell of food, but this time it was fresh and mouthwatering, even if it was German. He forced himself past the appetizing miasma and crouched low to the ground to move toward the main room of the apartment.

The furniture was stacked and covered with tarps. He assumed the residents had packed up and moved after the Germans occupied the city. Wise people, and he hoped they found somewhere safe to ride out the rest of the war. After he made sure no one was lurking on the ground floor he continued to the foot of the stairs. The voices were coming from above, the street-facing room to the right. He ascended slowly; the benefit of approaching in wolf form meant that he wasn't heavy enough to make the risers creak underfoot.

He was almost too the second floor when he heard one of the Germans quietly exclaim. There was a shuffling sound as they repositioned themselves.

"Look. They must have another truck coming."

"Impossible. They are fortunate to have one truck full of petrol. No one can afford two. Perhaps they are heading to the train station."

The first soldier laughed. "They are stupid, but not quite that stupid, I'm afraid. We'll wait until they're on the move and we'll pick them off like a shooting gallery. Simple. Straight shots." He chortled. "They won't even have time to draw their weapons."

The other man said, "If they are walking away from us, we can pick them off one by one from the back. The ones at the front won't even know what is happening."

They both laughed. Kenneth risked sticking his head around the door and saw that both men were crouching on either side of the window. One of them was holding a Karabiner 98k rifle just out of sight, but Kenneth could tell the man would have no hesitation using it. There was just something about the way some men held a weapon that made it obvious they relished the chance to cause pain with it.

Kenneth crept past the doorway to the next room in the corridor. The door was slightly ajar, so he nudged it with his snout until it began to swing open. He stepped inside and hunched down just beyond the threshold. The sunlight coming from the sniper's room fell across the hall so he would see the shadow of anyone approaching. Once he was in position, he used his tail to knock the door against the wall.

"*Hirnlose ochse...* I told you to close that door."

"I did."

"Go close it now. I can't afford to be distracted. I could have blown a hole in their suitcases and the bastards would have scattered. Go!"

Kenneth braced himself to leap. The soldier's shadow appeared, and then he loomed in the doorway. He took a step back when he saw Kenneth in the room, but a cry of alarm was choked off in his throat. Kenneth pounced. The soldier brought up his arm to fend off the attack, and Kenneth bit down hard enough to drive his fangs through the sleeve and into flesh. The man gave a full-throated shout now, wailing as he brought his other hand up to club Kenneth on the head.

"Alois!" He wailed for his friend and swung his whole body around in an attempt to slam his attacker against the wall. "Alois! Wild dog! There is a wild dog!"

Kenneth growled and brought his back legs up. He pressed his feet against the soldier's midsection and dragged his claws down. The man's wailing intensified as he fell onto his ass. Kenneth heard the pounding of the other man's boots as he rushed to his cohort's aid. He heard a howl and a snarl as Anatole joined the attack, and the sniper fired a shot into the baseboard as he was tackled back into the room.

Blood was flooding Kenneth's mouth at that point, and he released his grip long enough to change his angle of attack. He snapped at the soldier's face, catching a glimpse of the man's terrified eyes. Red swarmed Kenneth's vision then, and he was grateful that the wolf had pulled down the veil before the truly gruesome attacks began. He was aware of his own body - the thudding of his heart, the bellows of his lungs, the warm copper flood in his mouth - and nothing else.

When he came back to himself, he was the only thing in the hall drawing breath. Blood marred his muzzle and the whole front of his chest. He turned and went into the side room where Anatole was crouching next to the sniper. He was in human form, dripping sweat, and there was a grisly slash across his chest. He spun toward the sound of Kenneth's entrance, but relaxed when he saw it was a friend.

"Took his gun, but the bastard had a knife. Nearly cut me open. I had to change to hold him back." He sniffed and stood up. "I'll take his uniform. Not feeling up for going wolfy just yet. You good? Your man...?"

Kenneth snuffed out a breath of air.

"Good man. You done good." He went to the window and peered out, so Kenneth did the same. They both crouched and looked across at the safe house. Suitcases were abandoned by the doorway and the entire street was empty of life. Kenneth looked at the other building across the way where they had seen the other snipers. No movement, but also no one waiting to take a shot. He had to hope Simon's group had been successful as well.

He dropped from the window and went back into the hall. His opponent was lying in an ever-growing pool of blood, his legs twisted underneath him and his arms splayed out to either side. He no longer had a face, and most of his throat was also missing.

Kenneth felt sick to his stomach and turned away from the mauling. It had to be done. If the man had been left alive, he would have done everything in his power to kill the Loupin pack.

He silently urged Anatole to hurry; the sooner they were quit of this place, the better.

CHAPTER FOUR

SIMON WAS encouraged to see the blood on Kenneth's fur when they got back to the house. Three wolves and one man dressed in a stolen, ill-fitting German uniform met up at the back door, and Simon gestured with his head for the other team to go in first. Kenneth trotted past the group gathered in the kitchen and went directly to the washroom, kicking the door shut behind him with one foot.

Simon had some war paint of his own, a splatter where he had locked onto the Kraut's leg and pulled it out from under him to make the soldier tumble down the stairs. He flew down the stairs and landed on top of the man to finish the job with a quick clamp on his throat and a twist of his head. If the bite itself didn't kill him, snapping his neck definitely finished the job. Leopold dispatched the sniper, and they took a few minutes to explore the German's nest to see if there were any supplies worth filching.

After Simon transformed, Gilles informed him that he'd gotten in touch with Sandrine and Didier. "They didn't see anyone pursuing them, but they've pulled off to give another look. I'm confident that Didier will pick up anything wily enough to get past Sandrine."

"Excellent." He looked at Anatole. "Did things go well on your end?"

"Marginally. I got a knife across the chest."

Simon narrowed his eyes. "Kenneth?"

"No. Wasn't his fault at all. In fact, he took out his man pretty brutally. Did a fantastic job of it."

"Good to know. Let me see the wound." Anatole undid the German jacket. "That'll scar. Oughta be good for some tail." He winked and patted the young man on the shoulder. "Go see Irene and have her stitch it up."

Anatole nodded and headed off. Simon took the clothes he'd discarded upon departure and slipped into them. To Gilles, he said, "Tell the others that the street is safe for now, but we're moving up our departure time. I want to be gone before anyone notices those sentries aren't there anymore."

"I'll let them know."

He went off, and Simon picked up Kenneth's discarded clothes. He carried them to the washroom, rapped his knuckles against the wood, and let himself in. Kenneth was standing in front of the sink washing the last of the blood from his chest, but there were still smears of it on his arms and shoulders. A memory intruded on Simon, the familiar feeling of being in this very situation with Philip. In those days he would have picked up a sponge and helped him wash the last of the blood away, pressing up against him as he squeezed the sponge to let water cascade down his lover's chest. Then he would follow the trail of water down Philip's stomach, feeling Philip press back against his erection as Simon wrapped a wet hand around the length of Philip's cock.

Simon dismissed the fantasy with a violent shake of his head, holding up the clothes. "Anatole said you did a great job out there."

"I let the wolf handle the rough stuff."

"Wise. We tend to flinch where the wolf can just go on instinct. The jerry would have done the same to us. Worse, maybe."

Kenneth nodded. "I'm well aware. It doesn't make it any easier." He wet the towel in the sink and brought it up to his chest. His nipples were hard, and Simon felt a tug below the belt at the sight of the other man's naked body. He knew he should leave and give Kenneth his privacy, but something caused him to remain.

"You seem shaken up. You were at Dunkirk so I know you've

killed before."

"Of course," Kenneth said. "This was different, though. It was an ambush. But like you said, no different than what they wanted to do to us." He leaned forward and pulled his lips back to show his teeth in the mirror. They were dark red at the gums, and he wet two fingers and reached into his mouth to scrub them clean. Simon watched with perverted interest, unable to separate what Kenneth was doing and what he *appeared* to be doing.

His heightened arousal was no surprise; he was always horny after a transformation. And if he'd been involved in violence while in wolf form, that lust was even stronger.

"We're leaving earlier than we'd planned," Simon said, focusing on the mission rather than the naked and dripping man in front of him.

"Right. Anatole and I found radio equipment. There might be someone on the other end waiting for an update. We should be out of here before they realized something has gone wrong."

Simon said, "Exactly right."

Kenneth smiled lopsidedly. "Not my first rodeo, Mr. Loupin. I'll be ready to go when it's time."

"Good." He stepped out of the bathroom and went down the hall to his bedroom. The wolf's libido was swirling in his mind, urging him to go back and take advantage of the beautiful Brit. He shut the bedroom door behind himself and leaned against it. He thought back to all the nights he'd lain in the bed wishing he had memories of Philip in the room to sustain him, but now for the first time he was grateful that he hadn't shared the room with his lover. He untied his pants and let them fall, bending his knees so they wouldn't hit the floor. He spit into his palm, gripped his tumescent cock, and began tugging until it was fully erect in his palm.

The wolf just needed a release. His adrenaline was spiked by the hunt and the kill. If Philip had been there, he would be kneeling on the floor with the head of Simon's cock in his mouth, tenderly cupping his balls, urging him to a cathartic orgasm. He didn't want romance or slow climax. He wanted to come quickly, he wanted it fast and nasty. He bared his teeth and growled, thrusting his hips forward.

He thought about young men he'd fucked before he met

Philip, the boys who hid their faces when they walked into the bars where they would find what they were embarrassed to want. They were always so eager to please. So hesitant at first. He loved watching the tension slide out of them as they gave in to their desires. Some wolves wouldn't have sex with humans, but he loved it. He loved knowing something they didn't, knowing he was a monster from fairy tales being invited into their beds.

No matter how much he tried to focus on the past, his mind wrapped back around to Kenneth's naked body. The water beading on muscle and toned flesh, the pink swirl of his victim's blood in the sink, and the plump semi-erection of his cock. He gave in to the fantasy, now committed only to his orgasm. He growled and imagined himself pushing Kenneth away from the sink and dropping to his knees. He would use his tongue to guide the head of Kenneth's cock into his mouth and close his lips around it before the other man could even think of protesting.

The image was powerful enough to push him to the edge of climax. He pressed his shoulders back against the door and moved his feet apart. He thrust his hips forward, squeezing his cock before brushing his palm against the tip. The orgasm built and then, right when he was on the cusp, someone knocked on the door behind him.

"Leave," he grunted.

"Are you sure?" Kenneth asked.

Simon's eyes snapped open. He could hear the desire in Kenneth's voice and knew what had drawn the other wolf to him: he could smell Simon's arousal. Simon breathed deeply and could smell Kenneth's. Their heightened states meant that even through the door he could pick up nuances of the Brit's odor. Simon turned and gripped his cock with one hand, the other flat against the door. He closed his eyes, lips puffing out as he imagined Kenneth on the other side. Wet and breathing hard, naked except for a towel held in front of himself as he listened to the sounds coming from Simon's room.

His breath was ragged and he felt the sweat rolling down his cheek. His face was burning as he imagined Kenneth on the other side listening to every grunt and growl. Was his cock getting hard? Was it swelling against the moist terrycloth of the towel he was using to cover himself? Simon's hips rocked forward and he rose onto the balls of his feet as if to push himself deeper into his lover. He hadn't fucked anyone since Philip died, but now he had the urge to pull the door open and grab Kenneth. Slam the door and press him against it, crowd up against him, work his cock between the tight cheeks of the Brit's ass, and... and...

Simon closed his hand around his cock as it throbbed. He arched his back and grunted, sagging forward with his cheek against the door. When he recovered enough to think clearly, he opened the door with the hand that wasn't smeared with his come and was disappointed to see that the hallway was empty.

Ten minutes later he joined the others in the living room. Kenneth was consulting the map again, using his small finger to trace a road. Simon had dressed in casual civilian clothes so he wouldn't stand out, but that wasn't the most striking change. He'd spent the ten minutes in the bathroom shaving off the beard he hadn't touched since Philip died. Gilles was the first to look up and notice the change.

"You look good, sir. Almost like yourself again."

Kenneth looked up from the map and let his gaze linger on Simon's face before trailing down to the clothes. "It will get us out of the city, at least. We'll be traveling by a southerly route, moving counter-clockwise up to Meldeuses. I don't know that route as well as I'd like, so we'll have to make a few on-the-fly decisions once we're on the move. We'll find somewhere to change and let our wolves take the last leg. We managed to get a message to Sandrine; she knows to be on the alert, but they haven't had any cause for alarm."

"Good." Simon moved closer to the table. "The rest of you should get ready. Kenneth, you'll find clothes in the hallway closet. They should fit you."

They moved to go change clothes and Simon picked up the map. "Will it be safe?"

Kenneth stopped beside him. "Safe as this sort of thing gets. Are you worried about losing more men?"

"Always."

"Are you worried about Sandrine?"

"No. If they were being followed, she would know. And she wouldn't lie just to placate us. I think they're safe. But we're going to be running through very volatile territory with nothing between us and the Germans but a thick hide. And we have an unknown, untested man leading the way." He straightened and stared hard at Kenneth. "Forgive me if I'm blunt, but we haven't the luxury of being polite right now."

Kenneth took a step closer. "Maybe you'd like to test me."

Simon offered a smile that was more than half sneer. "Another time. If we survive. Go get dressed. We've stayed in this place far too long with a target painted on our back."

"Is that why you arranged the pack the way you did? Everyone relying on someone they know, except for you. So that if I do end up being unworthy..."

"Then I will be the only one to suffer."

Kenneth didn't look away. They held each other's gaze for a long moment before Kenneth drew a deep breath and held it. Simon had washed up, but he was well aware of what Kenneth smelled below the soap and aftershave. Kenneth's lips curled into a slight grin as he finally turned away and went to retrieve his clothes. Simon watched him go and focused on the map. He hoped to have the route memorized by the time everyone else was ready, and it was a long way to Isles-les-Meldeuses.

CHAPTER FIVE

WHEN THEY were walking distance to their destination, Sandrine left the truck and its supplies in a barn that appeared to be abandoned. Didier remained behind to guard it while she walked into town to make contact with the local resistance members. She knew there had to be some sort of presence, but they would be wary of a stranger asking the wrong questions. She knew that if someone started sniffing around for them in Paris or Monthyon she would have responded with a knife between their ribs. It was just safer than taking a chance on a spy.

Now they needed a place to stay and contacts they could trust, but first she needed to prove that she could be trusted. It would have helped if Kenneth could have sent word ahead to be on the lookout for them, but they were fighting against time. For the mission to succeed they would have to take some risks.

She had changed clothes in the truck, now wearing an ankle-length dress under two sweaters and a heavy coat. Her hair was pinned back in an attempt to make her look dowdy, but instead it highlighted the sharpness of her cheekbones and the sharp line of her jaw. Her eyes were large and dark, a feature that her mother once said made her look like a church mouse. No one would mistake her for anything quite so innocent, no matter what clothing she wore.

Isles-les-Meldeuses was a gorgeous choice for hiding out. The western approach was miles of empty road flanked on either side by woodland thick enough it might as well have been a leafy green wall. They could place sentries all along the approach to the commune in wolf form to watch for any approaching hostiles. The rest of the town was surrounded by a bell-shaped curve of La Marne, with only two bridges if the map could be believed. She didn't throw around her trust easily, but Kenneth Mackay had definitely found them a perfect place to hole up for a while.

Sandrine took in the town as she walked across its western border. She was looking for public houses, which afforded the perfect opportunity to meet clandestinely. Due to their frequency of bars and pubs, many believed the resistance was made up of drunkards and weak-willed individuals who existed on the fridges of polite society. It was propaganda meant to dissuade people from joining up. The truth was that every resistance member needed courage and fortitude in order to make the first step to joining the insurgency. They were asked to cut ties from their past lives, to lie to friends and family members or simply cut them out of their lives entirely. They made themselves an island so they couldn't endanger those they loved while they were fighting to free their country. If that wasn't bravery, then Sandrine didn't know the meaning of the word.

The majority of businesses she passed were closed because the owners couldn't afford to restock and their customers couldn't afford to eat there even if the shelves were full. The first open pub she found was a nondescript building of white stone. Six tables were set up on a fan of brick pavement outside but no one had taken advantage of them. She paused on the threshold to take off her gloves and took the opportunity to observe the men seated within. The bartender glanced up but betrayed no unusual interest in her arrival. A man near the back looked at her from under the brim of his fedora long enough that his partner turned around to see what had captured his attention.

Sandrine smiled to the trio and walked to the bar. "Could I trouble you for a glass of water, please? I'm extremely parched."

"Water's not free. Not even for women."

"Oh, I intend to pay." She reached into her clutch and presented her ration card with a flourish. "With ice, if you would be so kind."

The bartender cut his eyes toward the men in the corner and turned around to fill a glass. The glance confirmed her suspicions. They were very lucky she wasn't with the Germans or else she would have already mowed them down. Instead she rested her hands on the bar while waiting for her drink and tapped her knuckle against the wood. Three dots and then a quick drag of her fingernail. Dot-dot-dot-dash. She repeated it a few times after she received her drink - "Merci!" - and sipped it with her other hand. Dot-dot-dot-dash.

One man's chair scraped across the hardwood floor as he stood up. Sandrine ceased the tapping and turned to face him. He took one step toward her and opened his mouth to speak, but she stopped him.

"Before we begin, please listen to some personal messages."

He stopped and looked at his friend. She had just echoed the opening code for the subversive radio station, a cue that vital information was about to be transmitted to the resistance. It was innocent enough on its own, but if these men were who she thought they were, they would recognize it.

The man still seated said, "You listen to Radio Londres?"

"When I must. You recognized my tapping."

"V."

"For victory," she said. "Sorry we couldn't arrange a proper meeting, but we're a bit crunched for time. I'm Sandrine Loupin. Our cell was originally based in Monthyon until a few months back."

"Patrick Loupin's group," the bartender said. "We've heard of them."

Sandrine smiled at the attempt to trip her up. "That is not his name. Since he is dead there is no harm in saying it: Philip. He was murdered in an attack that we now believe was part of a bigger plot."

The bartender said, "We've had a few groups come through here to rest for the night. They said the same thing. Sudden attack, fleeing to somewhere safer. It seemed odd, but we just thought the Germans were cracking down everywhere."

"We have intel from London that says otherwise. They're clearing house in this specific area. Our cell has been enlisted to see if we can find out why."

The man who had remained seated finally stood up. "I'm Sylvester, this is Urbain. The man behind the bar is Fabien."

"Sandrine. We were hoping to find a place here where we could set up a base of operations."

The men looked at each other before Fabien said, "The Bouchard farm has been empty since Harold left. No one would bother them out there."

Sylvester nodded. "It's a good site. When do the rest of your people get here?"

"Soon," Sandrine said. "Can you take me to the farm? I'd like to see for myself if it's worthy."

Urbain nodded and stepped forward. "I can take you. The people here know me, so they won't question you too much."

He led her outside. Next to the bar was a narrow lot blocked off by an iron fence and filled with discarded milk crates, old tires, and other refuse. He freed two bicycles from the mess and handed them to Sandrine so she could stand them on the sidewalk. "Hope you know how to ride."

"I'm better on foot," she said, meaning on all four of her paws, "but I know my way around one of these." She was wearing a skirt, so she took a moment to gird up her loins. She pushed the front of the material between her legs, then wrapped it around her thighs to tie the ends into a knot. It felt like a diaper, but it would prevent the skirt from tripping her up. Urbain waited for her to be ready before shoving off, and she hopped onto the seat to follow him.

He led her east through town, riding slowly until he realized she would be able to keep up with him. The town reminded her greatly of Monthyon; narrow roads, lots of foliage, and houses that were hidden behind trees or bushes. It was a very private place and, more importantly, easily fortified. It was the sort of place Philip would have found for them, and her estimation of Kenneth's choice rose even higher.

Urbain led her through town and down a narrow pathway that took them close enough to the river that she could smell the water. He skidded his foot along the gravel to stop in front of a latched gate she wouldn't have seen if he didn't step right up to it and fumble with the lock. She kicked down the stand of her bike and joined him just as he got the lock off.

"Harold and Sarah Bouchard are the owners." He tucked the lock into the pocket of his overalls. "They had family in America, and they made it out before everything went to hell. They won't be back until the war is over, and by then I doubt you'll still need this place."

"Not likely," Sandrine said. She didn't know what she would do when the war ended. Fighting gave her a purpose, and the idea of going back home was almost depressing. She wanted the war over, of course, but she couldn't expect a life as thrilling as the one she led now once Hitler and his foot soldiers were finally dealt with.

It was a problem for another day, she decided. Urbain led her down the dirt path on the other side of the gate until she could see the farmhouse around the gentle rise of land. It wasn't much to look at, but that was fine as long as it was also difficult to look at. She scanned the surrounding area. They would be visible from the water, but the trees made them invisible from the road. It also made the road invisible to them, but Simon would definitely have eyes in place to make sure they were protected.

"It will work perfectly, Urbain."

"We may be a small group, but we're here if you need an extra pair of hands."

Sandrine sighed. "There's a war on, Urbain. We need all the hands you've got." She started up the winding drive. "C'mon. I want to make sure the place is habitable before the rest of my group gets here."

Simon and Kenneth crouched next to the road in their wolf forms, the branches hanging low enough to shield them from passing vehicles. They waited until the final truck was entirely out of sight before emerging to continue their journey. Wolves weren't entirely unheard of in France, but they had been mostly eradicated since the late twenties. Simon didn't expect the Germans to know that or to fully comprehend the significance of seeing two wolves prowling together through the woods, but he preferred safety to regret.

It was sixty kilometers to Isles-des-Meldeuses, a distance they could easily cover in a few hours if they weren't forced to take cover every five minutes. He let Kenneth take the lead since he knew the way better, and letting the wolf mindlessly follow someone else gave his mind the chance to wander. He thought of Philip and their first mission together, before they became lovers. Simon had been a brand-new recruit to the resistance, unsure of himself or the people with whom he was now throwing in his lot. He was an orphan and had nothing tying him to home.

He was born in Charleval, a tiny commune in northern France. His parents died when he was a teenager, not long after he began shifting, so he was sent to live in an orphanage. He wasn't trained to control the wolf and quickly learned that the beast didn't take kindly to being ignored and suppressed. If he went too long without transforming it would happen in his sleep. He would find himself outside in the woods, naked and smeared with mud and blood. He quickly earned a reputation as a troublemaker and suffered the lash for what the caretakers deemed flagrant disregard for the rules.

"You cannot go out at night," they would say, "the groundskeeper has seen wolves around here! Do you want to get eaten by a wolf?"

He finally ran away when he was fourteen. The wolf took him all the way to Paris, where he stole clothes from a line and found shelter in a building that had been abandoned since the Great War. He eventually found work apprenticing in a newspaper office. It kept him busy and gave him enough money for food, and that was enough until he figured out something else. He was twenty years old when the war broke out. Reporters and photographers disappeared overnight to sign up, so he was promoted to general whatever-the-editor-needs.

He was the one who discovered someone was breaking in after hours to use the printing materials. He didn't tell his boss because the man was sympathetic to the Germans, and because he wanted the credit for capturing the thieves. The break-ins occurred only on Tuesdays and Thursdays, so he locked himself in the offices and waited.

It didn't take long. The first night, a Tuesday, he heard the lock being jimmied a few minutes before midnight. He had armed himself with a length of pipe and a knife, crouched in one of the cupboards that ran along the back wall. He listened intently and counted three intruders. He could handle three people, he told himself. He pushed open the cupboard door, howled a fearsome war cry, and fell flat on his face. His legs burned with pins and needles from being stuffed in the cupboard. In the darkness he could see the intruders looming over him. He swung the pipe in their general direction.

"Stop! Thieves!"

"We're not thieves." The voice belonged to a woman, which surprised him. She smelled of dirt and grass, crushed leaves, the oaky scent of a wood fire... She moved to kneel down beside him. "And you are no ordinary copy boy, are you?"

He was breathing hard enough that he could detect another scent underneath everything else. She was a wolf, and so were the others. His righteous anger faded into curiosity.

"Wolves?"

"We just need to use the machinery to print a few pamphlets. It could save lives."

Simon got to his feet and leaned against the counter as the feeling returned to them. "There's a lamp on the table over there. If M. Flandin sees the light he'll assume I'm working late or cleaning."

One of the shadowy figures moved to light the lamp. Its soft amber glow filled the room and revealed the three intruders. The men were wrapped in heavy jackets and had caps pulled low over their eyes. The woman wore a wool shirt and trousers held up by a pair of suspenders. Her hair was tucked underneath her cap but a few strands had tumbled down to frame her face.

"We won't come back after tonight," said the man, "but we don't have time to find another place. We have to get these pamphlets printed or our friends will die."

Simon knew he was at a crossroads, but there was no hesitation in his mind. "I will help you."

The woman put her hand on his arm. "This isn't a decision to be made lightly."

"I know. I'm not." He picked up the lantern and moved past the first man. "I will show you how to use the printers properly. You've been leaving messes. If you were better at it, no one would ever have known you were here."

"We'll be in your debt, my friend."

"My name is Simon."

The man offered his hand. "I am Philip. This is Irene and Didier. Welcome to the pack."

Kenneth turned and yelped at him, drawing Simon back to the present. He'd been allowing the wolf to guide him and was unsurprised to find he didn't recognize the area they were in. He followed Kenneth off the road and crouched under a bow of branches. He could feel the vibration of the trucks in the ground; it was going to be a big vehicle or a bunch of small ones. He and Kenneth got as low to the ground as possible, their haunches touching in the shadows, and they waited until the path was clear again.

CHAPTER SIX

SANDRINE RADIOED Didier and told him the name of the pub she'd found and the men who would be there. He passed the information on to the next group, and they would pass it to the next. Someone would be waiting for Kenneth and Simon at the edge of town to bring them in. While they waited for the others to arrive, she and Urbain prepared the farmhouse. There were three bedrooms, and she told Urbain to arrange them so everyone would have a place to sleep. She felt bad about making a mess of the home for the people who were mostly likely coming back for it one day, but needs must.

She cleared out the dinner table to use the space for a strategy room. She was carrying the kitchen chairs out to the barn when Didier arrived with the men from the pub. She nodded a greeting to them and continued where she had been going as he parked the truck. By the time she got back Didier and Sylvester had gotten out of the vehicle. Sylvester was walking toward the house, but Didier altered course to speak with her.

"Fabien is remaining behind at the bar until Kenneth and Simon get here. Didn't want to raise suspicions." She said nothing. "Already reverting back to the strong silent thing, eh? Shame. I'm going to miss your beautiful, methodic voice."

She snorted. "Sylvester sent out messages to the rest of his cell. They've been coming in one or two at a time. Urbain is confirming they are who they say they are."

Didier helped her rearrange the chairs in the barn. There was a dearth of space, but he was a master of working with what he had. As he stacked and rearranged what she had already done, she walked to the barn door and put her hands in her pockets. Urbain left the house and trotted down the driveway. He opened the gate, spoke to someone on the other side, and stepped back to let them in. Sandrine was about to look away when the woman appeared.

She looked at be about Sandrine's age, with white-blonde hair and an ashen complexion. Even from a distance her eyes looked black. She wore a blue turtleneck under a man's blazer. Her pants were also men's, cinched tight with a belt. The other woman's gaze landed on Sandrine and didn't waver, almost as if she had expected to find something of interest in that very spot. The wind shifted and Sandrine took a deep breath. Above the crisp emptiness of the winter afternoon she caught a hint of the woman's natural scent. It was earthy and rich, and reminded her of coffee. Her mouth watered and she told herself it was just the longing for caffeine. She breathed in again, but the wind had shifted.

"You are so amiable, Sandrine." Didier was standing right behind her. She hadn't noticed his approach, and his voice made her jump. "Making friends wherever you go."

Sandrine turned to glare at him. He smirked and walked back into the barn. When she looked again, Urbain was already leading the blonde woman into the house. Sandrine waited to see if the woman looked at her again, but she was focusing on whatever Urbain was telling her. She declared the moment over and went to find Didier.

"We have the house mostly converted to a base. Any word on the others?"

Didier said, "Everyone is on schedule last I heard. Simon and Kenneth should be here in about three hours."

"Good. In the meantime, Sylvester and Urbain can tell us what they know."

Sylvester shrugged. "I don't know much, but perhaps between us..."

"Anything will be better than the information we have now," Sandrine said. "Inside. I don't want too many people hanging around even if we're not in plain view. Didier, put this truck in the barn. If there's no room, knock down one of the stalls."

"Isn't this someone's home?"

"And if they make it through the war with only a bit of damage to their barn, they will consider it miraculous. Go."

Didier snorted. "I liked it better when you didn't talk."

"When Simon gets here, I'll leave the speeches to him. Until then I'm his mouthpiece."

They moved into the house and Sylvester took a moment to examine the work they'd done. "Not bad. You did a nice job out here." Urbain came downstairs and offered his compatriot a nod. "Fabien and I sent out a few notes while we were waiting for your friends to show up. Don't know when or if we'll hear back, but if anyone else has noticed something going on in this area, we'll know about it soon enough."

"Information is key," Didier said. "They fired a few shots and we all scattered like rats."

"Well, we're not scattering anymore," Sandrine said. "Someone killed Philip just to scare us into running away. They succeeded for a while, but we're not running anymore."

Simon and Kenneth transformed outside of Meldeuses and met up with members of Sylvester's cell. They were escorted to the Bouchard farm, where they reunited with the rest of the pack. Sandrine was so grateful to return the yoke of leadership to Simon that she practically vanished into the wallpaper as soon as he walked in the door. He took a moment to greet everyone to prove to himself they were all safe and intact, but also as a show of gratitude. Every one of them could have decided to turn tail and run while he was busy wasting rations getting drunk. He didn't deserve their loyalty. Philip earned that trust, had proven time and again he would be there for them no matter what happened. Now Simon had to show he was a worthy successor.

When he got to Sylvester, he extended his hand. "I'm Simon Loupin. I'm the leader of this group."

Sylvester introduced himself and the others with him. "Your

girl did a good job while she was waiting for you to get here. You obviously trained her well."

"No one trained Sandrine. She was a weapon. All I taught her was how to eat with utensils and not growl at strangers on the street."

Sylvester chuckled and scanned the room for Sandrine, but he couldn't find her. Simon saw her sitting between a lamp and a window, making use of the shadow there to prevent anyone from paying attention to her. He didn't tell Sylvester where she was. If she wanted him to know she would have revealed herself to him.

"Now that we're all here," Sylvester said, "perhaps the time has come to share what we know."

"Kenneth will take care of that part. What he knows comes direct from British Intelligence."

Kenneth moved to stand next to Simon as he repeated the news he'd given Simon's pack when they first met. To Sylvester, he said, "Did you have any interaction with the other cells who fled after the attacks began?"

"A few." He pointed to a few of the marks on the map. "The ones here and here. We have a few farms with food stores and animals that can be slaughtered. These cells were nearby, so we were able to trade with them from time to time. I'm surprised we never crossed paths. You were stationed, what, twenty kilometers from here."

Simon said, "Give or take." He decided not to satisfy Sylvester's curiosity. The truth was Philip wanted to limit their interaction with non-*canidae* cells. The ability to transform into wolves was a vital tool in their arsenal, and they didn't want to cripple themselves by aligning with someone who didn't know the secret.

When he decided Simon wasn't going to elaborate, Sylvester continued. "We wondered where they had gone, but we just assumed they were discovered and had to move."

"That's how this plan worked. No one questions it if a resistance cell just up and disappeared. The attacks allowed you to believe you were fortunate, you were surviving, when actually you were playing right into their hands. You did exactly what your enemies wanted. Any actual loss of life, as tragic as it was, would be discounted as, ah…" He glanced at Simon out of the corner of his eye.

Simon said, "Collateral damage. An unexpected bonus. They got us out of town and took a few of our lives in the process."

"Yes," Kenneth said. "Since everyone fled, this area has been unprotected and unobserved. The Germans could've been doing anything in the past six months and we'd be none the wiser. That's why we've come back. Sylvester, have your men seen or heard anything that might be cause for alarm?"

"The whole cursed war," Urbain said. He was standing near the door, arms crossed over his chest. "Trucks coming and going all the time, soldiers posted 'just to keep an eye on things,' taking over train stations and commandeering anything they might possibly need at some point in the future. They're like an infestation. But specifically? No. There's been nothing."

An older blonde woman who had been sitting silently on the divan lifted her hand. She was dressed against the cold in a fur-lined jacket and a heavy sweater, her hair mostly covered by a hat with earflaps. She looked like a grandmother on her way to church. Sylvester nodded to her.

"Easter Reynolds. Go ahead."

"Well, what Urbain said is true, there have been trucks and soldiers since the war began. But one thing has changed. The trucks and soldiers come from the southwest, but they do not return from the north. More and more come and none of them ever come back."

Simon said, "From Paris to the area they cleared out. They're building up forces."

"But why?" Fabien said. "There's nothing of value up there."

"Not yet." Kenneth was staring at his hand-drawn map, rubbing one thumb over his bottom lip. "They're passing through here on the way to someplace else. What do they do when they're here?"

"Whatever they want," Sylvester said. "They take our food, our vehicles, our water. But Miss Reynolds is correct. We rarely see the same men twice. Once they are north, they stay there."

Simon moved closer to Kenneth so he could see the map as well. "If these are the cells that were flushed out, and the troops are moving in through here, it is reasonable to assume the focus of their attention is somewhere in this area." He tapped the paper on an area he vaguely remembered as being nothing but empty farmland. "They're preparing something there."

Kenneth nodded. "Then it is up to us to discover what it might be."

CHAPTER SEVEN

"...COULD BE anything," Sylvester was saying. "Railroads, barracks, farmland. There are many reasons the Germans might have wanted this area cleared of resistance. Hell, they might have just wanted to flush us into a larger city so they could pick us off more easily."

"We did have to deal with an attack before we left Paris," Simon said, "but this feels larger. It feels more purposeful."

Sandrine had listened to their debating long enough. She slipped through the crowded drawing room without attracting any attention to herself. The voices of the others faded as she went into the kitchen. Everyone was focused on the mission, but she knew the more pressing issue was food. They were a huge group and soon everyone would want something to eat. It was hard enough feeding everybody when they were in Paris and there was always garbage to be scrounged. She and Didier had moved in some of the food stores, and she went through it to see what they stretch into a meal for thirty

She smelled the other woman before she saw her. The blonde she'd been so strangely transfixed by came into the kitchen from upstairs. Her blazer was gone and she was barefoot. She stopped when she saw Sandrine at the dinner table but proceeded after a moment of contemplation. When she was a few feet away she stopped and looked into the living room.

"Are they still talking?"

Sandrine nodded.

"So much information at once, it… makes my head… loud. That's the wrong word. Ideas and theories, you know? Questions without answers. I prefer to have it all laid out for me when people have had a chance to arrange it in a way I can understand." She moved to put her hands in her pockets, remembered she wasn't wearing her jacket, and crossed her arms in front of herself. "I'm Minuit. Min."

"Sandrine."

"Hi." She came closer and put her hands on the back of the chair. "We have food."

Sandrine raised an eyebrow.

"We grow a lot, but we still ration so we can have stockpiles. So we can help people who come through if they need it. I just thought you should know we don't expect you to feed us. We can offer you food, if you want."

Sandrine said, "Simon will make that decision."

Min said, "Okay."

There was something off about the girl, but Sandrine couldn't quite pick out what it was. She spoke French incredibly well, but there was an accent she didn't recognize coloring everything she said. Sandrine decided it wasn't a mystery that needed solved right then.

"There are nineteen members of our cell. We cannot all stay here without drawing suspicion."

Min nodded. "Sylvester has people working on that. People are willing to offer their basements and barns. Hope that's okay."

Sandrine nodded. Everyone in the cell was accustomed to sleeping rough. If necessary a few of them could spend the night as a wolf and find someplace outside to bed down.

"You don't talk much."

"When I have something to say. I had to talk a lot more than I'm comfortable with to get our cell up here."

"So you're stockpiling, too."

Sandrine smiled almost without realizing it. "I suppose."

"Okay. Do you need help putting this away?"

Sandrine nodded, and Min helped her unpack one of the boxes. There was still something about the other woman that made her uneasy, but it was too vague for her to grasp. It was like a barely-heard whisper from another room, or the name of someone she'd once known years before. She could see the shape where the answer was supposed to be, but it had no edges for her to dig into. It was a mystery that could wait for another day.

"Have you seen much fighting?"

"Some."

"We've been lucky. No one bothers us much here."

"Sorry to bring this to your door."

Min shook her head. "No. We welcome the opportunity. We do not want Germans marching through our town or shooting at us, but we are more than willing to do our part. If that means giving up our beds for a month or three, if that means having crackers for dinner so someone else can have soup, then we are ready to make those sacrifices."

Sandrine said, "I do not like soup. If it comes to that, I will take your crackers and you can have my soup."

Min smiled. "Spectacular. We are making friends already."

Leopold came in from the living room. Sandrine set her face in a neutral expression, only then becoming aware of how animated she'd been. Leopold looked at Min and brushed past Sandrine to get a glass of water from the tap. Min saw what he was doing and stopped him.

"That's not attached yet. I'll get you some from the pump outside."

"Oh, it's not necessary..."

She was already halfway to the door. "It must be done anyway. I'll tell Baldwin it needs to be done before we leave tonight. It was a pleasure to meet you, Sandrine."

"Mm."

The door smacked shut against the frame. Leopold watched the space where the other woman had been and smiled at Sandrine. "It was a 'pleasure'? Girl like the sound of silences?"

"It's a virtue you might do well to learn, Leo," Sandrine said. "What did they decide?"

"We're going to send a group up north to see if we can find anything."

She furrowed her brow. "They're just going in blind?"

Leopold shrugged. "It's all we can do right now. Simon and the Brit are going to take a couple of us around the north country, and Sylvester asked for volunteers to go around to some of the communes that got cleared out, see if anyone is willing to talk."

It was a good plan. They couldn't risk the other cell becoming suspicious, and Simon's plan allowed their pack to transform without making Sylvester's people think they were hiding something. They were all playing a pivotal role, and the Meldeuses cell didn't have to know the Loupins were doing their part on four legs.

"Where does he want me?"

"Here, holding down the fort."

Sandrine nodded. She knew there were others who would bristle at being told to stay home, but she knew how vital the farmhouse was. All their supplies, all their members who weren't going off into battle, everything vulnerable. It was her duty to make sure the sanctuary remained when the field units returned. It wasn't a responsibility she took lightly. She walked to the window and looked outside. The sun was mostly set, and the enclosed yard was awash with shadows. Min had placed a large bucket under a hand pump in the middle of the yard, and Sandrine watched as she gripped the handle. The metal shrieked as she lifted the pump and pushed it back down. The strain was obvious, but the woman didn't waver. She was strong.

To get her mind off its current track, Sandrine said, "What do you think of Mackay?"

"The Brit?" Leopold shrugged. "He's all right, I suppose. Could have been sent a lot worse. Glad they sent another wolf. Could've been a nightmare if we had to hide ourselves from him."

Sandrine muttered her approval. "And the girl?"

"What girl?"

Sandrine gestured with her chin.

"What about her?"

"Something," Sandrine murmured. "Can't tell what. You didn't pick up anything?"

Leopold snorted. "Oh, I definitely sensed something. But it had nothing to do with whether or not she's trustworthy."

Sandrine sneered at him.

"Nah, I'm only teasing. It'll be good. You haven't had anyone since... what was her name, the singer? Vivienne?"

Sandrine unconsciously licked her lips at the mention of her ex-lover.

"You want my opinion of her?" He joined her at the window and put his hands on her shoulders. He watched Min pump for a moment and then playfully clapped Sandrine on the side of her head. "Go. Do it. Don't worry if she likes guys or not. Just tell her it's war and you don't know when you'll have another chance to feel alive. Women love that stuff."

"The sort of women you attract, you mean," Sandrine said. "Not sure I'm quite that desperate."

He clapped her on the side of the head again. She stomped on his foot and he hissed. "That actually hurt. You're mean when you aren't getting laid."

"There are knives in this room, Leopold."

He stepped back without assaulting her again. "You asked my advice, Sandrine. I gave it. This war is more than just stopping the Germans. It's about being free to live our lives. Taking a night off to pursue your happiness is just as important as sabotage and fighting."

She crossed her arms over her chest and watched Min as she finished filling up the bucket. "Perhaps I will. Once I discover what it is she's hiding."

The farmhouse could comfortably hold five people. It could uncomfortably hold ten. So Simon decided that thirteen of them could stay there. Five volunteers were assigned to stay in the basement, coming out only for security patrols. It wasn't said aloud in mixed company, but it was implied that those five would be in wolf form for the duration of their stay in Meldeuses. It was a way to save space and resources, since the wolves didn't eat as much and didn't need anywhere near as much space. Four people would share the master bedroom, and then two people could bunk together in the children's rooms.

Kenneth wanted people camped out in the drawing room, but

Sylvester advised against it. They didn't want too many people moving in and out of the house. The remaining four members of the Loupin pack would be bivouacked at houses throughout the commune. Their hosts were strategically located so they would see any incoming German transports.

Sylvester and his people left so Simon's cell could settle in. Once the humans were gone, Simon gathered everyone in the drawing room again.

"Armand, Jerard, Gilberte, Umber. You four will be posted at the cardinal points of the commune's map. If you see any enemy movement, either coming into Meldeuses or just passing by, get here as quickly as possible. If you can transform into your wolves to make the trip, more's the better. We don't want our neighbors getting suspicious of too many people coming and going. In fact, wolf form as often as possible.

"Leopold, Ambrose, Ivonne, Maxime. I want you to be absolutely certain you are comfortable being your wolves for the long haul. I don't know how long we'll be here, but if it's more than a month we can switch out a rotation so you can be yourselves again."

Leopold said, "I once went six months as a wolf to get into one of those godawful camps. When the cause is just enough, I don't mind a little brain soup."

"We can't afford much brain soup," Kenneth said. "We need everyone here to be on the absolute top of their game. If any of you feel yourselves slipping, or if you suffer loss of time beyond what is normal for you, let us know immediately and we'll get you out of the basement."

The four volunteers nodded their understanding, but Simon knew them well enough to know they would only request reprieve under the direst of circumstances. He would have to be sure they were rewarded for their sacrifice when this nonsense was all said and done. If that day ever came. He looked over the faces of his pack, their new combined cell, and thought about what they had been before France became occupied by evil. Doctors, farmers, bookkeepers. He knew for a fact that Irene had been a seamstress before she was forced to become a medic. In a way he was sad she would have to go back to it; she was an excellent doctor, but he couldn't imagine anyone allowing her to practice in peacetime.

"We should take tonight to rest," Sylvester suggested. "You've all come a very long way and you need to settle in. Acclimate. If we ever need to meet with more than a handful of us, we can do it at my pub. It's less conspicuous, and I have enough ration cards to cover anyone who shows up. Let's try to keep our congregating to a minimum, though."

Simon said, "Agreed." Sandrine had returned to the room without him noticing. She stood against the door to the kitchen, arms crossed over her chest. "Sylvester, thank you for your hospitality."

"You would have done the same for us. We'll get out of your hair so you can settle in."

Sylvester's people left in stages, some through the front while others went through the wooded area at the back of the farm's land. Once they were gone, Simon pulled aside the four pack members who had agreed to be stationed on the outskirts of the commune.

"Follow as many of them as you can before going to your posts. I want to trust them. I very nearly trust them. But I would like to be absolutely certain our trust isn't misplaced."

Kenneth said, "I assure you, they were vetted by our top intelligence."

"That's enough for ninety percent," Simon conceded. "I'd like to get a full one hundred. You would do the same in my place."

Kenneth nodded, albeit reluctantly.

Simon sent the four off to transform and motioned for Sandrine to follow him into the kitchen. "You obviously wanted to ask me something."

"The blonde," she said, "in the blue turtleneck."

"What about her?"

She shook her head. "I don't know. I was hoping you could fill in the blanks. She's... wrong somehow. She makes me itchy."

He laughed quietly. "Itchy?"

"It's hard to explain."

"Perhaps you're attracted to her." He scoffed and shook his head. "No, I saw her. You're definitely attracted to her. This is something else?" She said nothing. "I didn't feel anything off about her, but I didn't spend much time with her. She was always either upstairs or out fetching water from the well."

Sandrine stared at him.

"You're right. That is a bit suspicious. I'll have someone keep a special eye on her."

She nodded her thanks and he started to walk away. He stopped at the door when she said his name, but when he turned to face her she was looking out the window.

"The way you sounded in there. It was like before. Before you spent your days in bars. You were a good leader today. Philip would have been proud."

He started to reply, but found his voice wouldn't cooperate. Besides, if anyone could understand the power of a silent nod, it was Sandrine. He pressed his lips together, nodded his head once, and went to corral the rest of the pack for their first night at the farmhouse.

CHAPTER EIGHT

THEY SPENT a week gathering what information they could. As wolves, Simon and Kenneth took a few of their members to the north to see what they could sniff out. Other members of the pack remained in human form and borrowed clothes from Sylvester's people so they could present themselves as farmhands or craftsmen looking for work. The story was the same all over: a mysterious group of German soldiers attacked in the night, descending on a certain household like a plague of locusts. The next morning, anyone who hadn't been killed in the attacks disappeared from town. Nothing seemed amiss in the aftermath except for a heightened presence of German troops.

And yes, most of them remembered when pressed, it did seem as if a lot of them were going north without ever coming back.

Sandrine kept a map at the house. When she received word from their informants, she would add a string to the map. One village said all troop movement was west-to-east, so she marked that. One villager pointed down a northerly road and said it had become Kraut Avenue. She marked that as well. There was a point on the map where all the strings would converge, and she knew that was where they would find the German's secret.

In the meantime, she tried to find ways to occupy her time.

Her initial toleration of being left behind began running out on the third day. She wanted to be doing something, not standing in one place on the off chance something bad happened. She needed action, something to quicken the blood before it turned to sludge in her veins. She hadn't even transformed since they arrived, and the beast was itching to explore its new territory.

She was dressing in Mrs. Bouchard's clothes, tying her hair back with a kerchief and going about the business of running a small farm. Sylvester told anyone who inquired that she was Sarah's cousin who had come to help out while the family was away. With the majority of the pack out hunting for information, the farm was practically empty save for the few who had remained to help her defend their new home. They were all suffering the same cabin fever she was, and she couldn't think of any way to ease their anxiety when she was also clawing at the walls.

Sandrine spent her copious free time reliving the night of the attack on Monthyon. She couldn't even remember how many attackers there had been, what they'd been wearing, or if any of them had spoken. She remembered black outfits: button-down shirts and pocketed pants heavy with the tools they had used to break into the house. Were they a special unit? Had they been enlisted by whoever was in charge of the mysterious project to the north? There was a chance the men who killed Philip had only been following orders.

Most of her thinking was done on the road. She walked the unmarked streets of Meldeuses to clear her head, wishing she could transform and run through the woods as the wolf. Maybe giving the primal side control of her body would give her analytical mind a chance to recall more details. The men had worn masks, but she wanted to remember the smells. She wanted to remember how it felt to have their blood spill on her skin.

Sandrine was so distracted that she didn't notice the bicycle until it was almost upon her. She tensed, tried to hide the fact she had fallen into a combat pose, and then truly relaxed when she recognized Minuit was the cyclist. The other woman wore a long black coat and a knit blue cap that left her blonde bangs exposed. Min smiled and skidded her foot along the asphalt to stop herself. She straddled the bike and lifted her chin as a greeting to Sandrine.

"Hello there. Out for a walk? It's okay, I remember you don't like to talk, so you can let me do all the talking."

"Thank you. But I don't mind. I am just getting out of the farmhouse. Any word from your men?"

"Nothing yet. Yours?"

Sandrine shook her head.

"Well, sometimes it takes a bit of work to earn trust. Double agents and triple agents aren't unheard of. We have to be wary of French sympathetic to the Nazis, as disgusting as that idea may seem."

"Disgusting. Not unheard of." She remembered the disquieted feeling she had gotten from Min at the farmhouse. "What are you hiding, Minuit?"

The other woman flinched. Her fists tightened on the handlebars of her bike, but the tension in her shoulders indicated flight rather than fight. The widening of her eyes also indicated she wanted to run away. She swallowed a lump in her throat and glanced over her shoulder to make sure the road was clear in case she did try to flee.

"I'm not a spy."

"Then tell me what you are."

Min was breathing heavily now, a cornered animal looking for a way out. "I am loyal to the cause. Please don't tell Sylvester or Simon that you're doubting that. They will exile me just for the speculation."

"You are lying about something."

"I am. But nothing that matters to the cause. You must believe me."

Min stepped closer to the bike. "Are you a lesbian?"

"What?"

"Simon is homosexual. So is Kenneth, I believe. And I've been known to share my bed with both genders. We don't care. If that is your secret, simply tell me."

Min was crying silently, tears rolling over her pale cheeks. "I cannot tell you my secret, Sandrine. I can only promise you that if the time comes, I will protect everyone in our cell with my life. That goes for you and your people as well. If slitting my wrists could cause one Nazi officer to die at the same time, I would beg you for a razor blade."

"Stop," Sandrine said. "I believe you."

Min broke down in full sobs then. Sandrine bristled and looked back the way she had come, then looked past Min. They were alone on the road, which was bordered on either side by dirty piles of snow. There was a thick bank of fog a few yards above their heads that made it look as if the world simply ceased to exist above the trees. Min's weeping was silent but every few seconds she would suck in a deep breath through her teeth. Sandrine knew someone else would offer comfort. Even Simon would have reached out and put a hand on her shoulder. But Sandrine didn't know how to do that.

"I am worse than what you say," Min finally said. "That is why I joined the resistance. I thought... I-I thought that by fighting these demons I would maybe be allowed into Heaven when I die."

Sandrine said, "I won't tell the others about your secret."

"Thank you." She sniffled and wiped her face with her coat sleeve. "I will come to the farmhouse tonight. I will cook dinner for those of you who have been forced to stay behind. It's the least I can do."

"That would be acceptable. We'll be grateful for the company."

"Sandrine... if I thought you would still look kindly upon me, I would tell you my truth in an instant. But I cannot."

"I understand. I will see you at the farmhouse tonight."

Min nodded and mounted her bicycle again. She shoved off and began pedaling down the street. Sandrine watched her go, wondering what secret she held. Was she a thief? Had she committed adultery or some other cardinal sin? Whatever the truth, Sandrine was determined to learn the truth before they left Meldeuses. She hadn't lied about trusting Min. If the Germans came, she had no doubt Min would fight as hard as any of them. But she was still going to keep an eye on the other woman until she knew enough to comfort her nerves.

Simon and Kenneth traveled over eighty kilometers to a commune called Chauny. According to Kenneth's intelligence, it was their best opportunity to find evidence of a large troop movement into the northern countryside. It was well-connected to

Paris by roads and rail, and it was surrounded by farmland that could be used to feed troops. There were Germans present, including an entire unit who had taken over every lodging Kenneth saw, but none of them gave a pair of wolves any undue attention. They spent the afternoon observing public houses and the non-uniformed people they encountered.

By the time twilight started casting long shadows over the streets, Kenneth had determined the sallow-faced young man sitting outside the train depot was a local resistance member. He had done little all day except read the newspaper and exchange idle chitchat with people who wandered by. Simon and Kenneth had eavesdropped on his conversations long enough to hear snippets of code talk.

"Colder every day, eh?"

"Spring has to come sometime."

"So they say, my friend, but I have my doubts."

They watched for two hours before the young man was actually put to work, revealing the bench upon which he sat was a shoeshine stand. He polished a German officer's boot, dipping the rag into a bucket of "melted snow" to give it an extra shine. Kenneth sniffed the air and could tell even from a distance that the bucket contained urine. He and Simon watched as the man grinned, dipped his rag into the disgusting bucket, and then rubbed it onto the German's boot until it shone.

"Tell your friends," the man said as the officer marched off. "I am always happy to make the German army look their finest!"

When an ordinary citizen approached, the young man moved the bucket away and used a small case of polish. It was then Kenneth was convinced they'd found a kindred soul. He signaled to Simon, who nodded his head in agreement. They left the depot behind and went to find a place to transform. There was no way to know if he was *canidae*, and it was dangerous enough approaching someone as a resistance member without adding the wolf to the equation.

They found a farm with laundry hung out to dry. They would borrow some clothes so they could meet with the shoeshine boy and return everything when they were finished. Kenneth leapt the fence and grabbed a pair of trousers and a shirt off the line. Simon did the same. They ran across the yard with the outfits hanging from their mouths and flapping like wings. Kenneth anticipated a shout from the house and possibly gunfire with every step, but they made it to a side road without incident.

Kenneth transformed as he was running, lifting his palms off the dirt road and slapping down a pair of human hands. The transformation rippled up his arms and through his torso, twisting and tearing him into another form until he could rise into an upright position. He pushed his arms out to the side as he trotted to a stop. Twisting at the waist to work out the kinks in his spine, he looked back to see Simon was also fully transformed.

Simon rose to his full height, sweat shining on his chest. His arms and legs were dusty and dirty from their long trek across the countryside, and his black hair hung thick over his forehead. Simon met Kenneth's stare head-on, daring him to look away. Kenneth decided he wouldn't be intimidated and instead lowered his gaze to the other man's cock. Simon was partially erect, as was Kenneth. It was sometimes a side effect of shifting, fortunate or not depending on the situation.

Kenneth finally huffed out a lungful of air, acknowledging his appraisal without giving final judgment, and bent down to pick up the clothes he'd dropped when his snout disappeared.

"We should get back to the station as soon as possible," he said as he stepped into the pants. "We don't know how long the boy will be there."

"He won't leave before twenty-one hundred. The last train comes in at 2050. I looked at the notice board while we were observing him."

"Excellent. Then we should have plenty of time. Still, I would prefer not to have this conversation on a crowded platform."

Simon nodded his head and cinched his pants shut. The clothes were a fairly good fit; Kenneth had learned how to eyeball clothing sizes due to his frequent need to grab something to cover himself up. He saw that Simon had the same skill. He had a feeling most, if not all, *canidae* taught themselves how out of sheer necessity. He finished buttoning his shirt and looked down at their bare feet.

"If we mean to pose as customers, I believe there is a rather large flaw in the plan."

"But not insurmountable. Come on."

He led the way back into town. He expected they would get a fair amount of odd looks, given their mismatched outfits and lack of footwear, but no one even looked their way.

"I suppose people looking destitute isn't as shocking as we would hope," Kenneth muttered.

Simon grunted. "I'm sure London has its share of ration cards and families going hungry in the street."

"I didn't mean..."

"I know you didn't. I'm still trying to shake the wolf. I have less control over my emotions right after a transformation."

It wasn't much of an apology, but it was more than Kenneth had expected. He decided not to press his luck and remain silent for the rest of their walk. Instead he thought of his feelings toward the acerbic French wolf. Simon was surly and irritable, and Kenneth normally preferred his partners to be a bit less explosive. He liked quiet and musical men. Literati who would put down their book for a quickie on a Saturday afternoon. He thought of the last lover he'd left behind in London. The sweet Alan, who had decided he'd finally gotten sick of waiting for Kenneth to get back from missions. Their final argument was eight months old, and he still found it a sore subject to revisit.

Instead he focused on the man who had introduced him to his true sexuality. For his formative years and well into adulthood, Kenneth had only bedded women. He loved their softness and the way they smelled, he loved their smiles and their gentle voices whispering in his ears. He liked running his thumb over a nipple and watching it become erect before taking it into his mouth, and he loved the feel of finally, slowly, sliding into a woman.

He was in the military when that changed. He was already an intelligence officer, already doing missions for the war effort. One such mission required him to gain access to a German politician's office. His plan required wining and dining the politician's male secretary. Kenneth was only offering friendship but, as the evening went on, it became clear that the secretary's inhibitions were getting progressively weaker. Suddenly he wasn't as shy about touching Kenneth's arm, his hand, or letting his hand linger on Kenneth's thigh.

It quickly became apparent that there was a way to blackmail the secretary into giving him everything they needed. After they left the bar, Kenneth guided the younger man into an alley. For king and country. For the cause. He kissed the young man expecting he would have to ignore the stubble or the roughness of the mouth. He guided the other man's hand to his belt, leaving no doubt what he was offering. They pulled apart with a gasp and Kenneth roughly placed the secretary's hand over the front of his trousers.

"Will you?" Kenneth had asked.

The boy got on his knees. Kenneth anticipated problems, formulated a lie about why he wasn't hard, but his penis was surprisingly cooperative. As soon as he felt the touch of the young man's tongue it began swelling. Kenneth put his hands in the secretary's hair and closed his eyes, bent his knees, and grunted quietly as he began thrusting. The boy turned out to be exceptionally skilled, or maybe it was just the shock of how enjoyable he found the experience, but Kenneth found himself throbbing through his orgasm in what he considered an embarrassing amount of time.

He looked down and saw the boy wiping his lips, looking up at him with hopeful eyes. It was incredibly dim in the alley, but he could still see the desire in his eyes. There was nothing to be gained by repaying what the boy had done. He had enough to serve as blackmail, but for some reason he pulled the boy up, undid his trousers, and sank to his knees. The secretary was incredibly thick and hard, and Kenneth had to close his eyes before he took it onto his tongue.

The boy whispered encouragement and suggestions to him, and soon warned that he was about to come. Kenneth let it happen, gagging slightly as it filled his mouth and forced him to swallow. He pulled back and coughed, shocked by what had just happened and even more startled to find he was hard again. His cock was standing up straight through his still-unfastened trousers, and he stuffed it painfully away.

"I know a place not far from here," the boy said in a rush.

Kenneth had the refusal ready on his tongue. Instead he stood up and took the boy's hand. "Show me where."

That night he lost his second virginity, something he hadn't even realized he possessed or would ever give away. Since then his lovers had been exclusively male. He assumed a day would come when he would entertain the thought of taking another woman to bed, but his wartime experience meant he'd been in close quarters with mostly men.

And he had to admit Simon Loupin was one of the most fascinating of those men. He vowed to learn more about his fellow wolf before he was sent off to another assignment.

CHAPTER NINE

THE LAST train of the day arrived as scheduled and spilled four people onto the platform. They were tired, defeated, and weary as they shuffled toward their homes without so much as a sideways glance at the shoeshine stand. Kenneth and Simon remained out of sight until the commuters were gone before they approached. The man was putting away his things and seemed not to hear them until Simon was standing right beside him. He didn't look up from his wooden box of polish and rags.

"Sorry, gentlemen," he said in German. "I'm finished for the day."

"Do we look like we require your professional services?"

He looked at Simon's feet, then twisted to look at Kenneth's. He slowly lifted his gaze and examined their faces. When he spoke again, it was in a much smoother French dialect.

"If you're going to rob me, the risk isn't worth the reward."

Kenneth said, "We're not going to rob you, friend. I couldn't help but notice the special mixture you were using for the German boots."

The slender man lowered his head to hide his smile. "It's the same as I use on everyone else's."

Simon had moved to block off the boy's exit route. "If you are urinating that much, perhaps you should see a physician."

The shoeshine boy laughed and stood up. "You have vivid imaginations, friends. What you're saying is vile. I would never do such a thing."

Kenneth said, "You should. Perhaps it would help wash off the blood of the innocents they tromp through every day they're squatting in our country." He held out his hand. "I'm Kenneth... Loupin. This is Simon Loupin. We'd like to speak with you, if we may, about anything unusual you might have seen the past six months."

He looked at Kenneth's hand, then eyed Simon warily. "How did you know about the water?"

"We watched you carefully."

"I never saw you."

"That's the point, no?" Simon said.

"I suppose." He finally took Kenneth's hand. "Jasper. You are not French."

Kenneth said, "Neither are you. But we fight for the same cause."

Jasper nodded. "Let's walk while we talk. Harder for eavesdroppers to listen in." He tucked his toolbox under his arm and started walking. Simon and Kenneth fell in beside him. "Unusual in the past six months. You realize the past few years, everything has been unusual. But I know what you mean. A lot of movement the past six months. Some on the rail but mostly by road. Trucks full of people and lots of boots that need shining. I've tried to get a little information here and there. People sit on my bench and forget there's a pair of ears kneeling in front of them. They tend to get gabby."

Simon scanned the street behind them to make sure they weren't being followed. "Anything that might interest us, as like-minded individuals?"

"They were sloppy, but not stupid. But yes, there's something happening up north."

Kenneth resisted the urge to punch the air. After a week of running around sniffing out leads, they might finally have found something.

Simon said, "We were based out of Monthyon until six months

ago. A group attacked us, set a bomb in our home, ran us out. We thought it was an isolated attack until Kenneth here showed up and told us differently. Seems the Germans were incredibly active for a while there. Knocked out close to a dozen cells, killed who they could, and sent the rest of us packing for safer climes. They just wanted us to be gone so we wouldn't see what you were seeing. Was there anything like that here?"

Jasper nodded. "Oh, yeah. Around the same time as you said, a troop moved in. They were based out of the old movie house. They rounded up a few people, had a public execution of one of 'em. Then they went away."

"Why didn't they get you?" Simon asked.

"They only got three actual members of the resistance. The rest were just citizens. Me and a couple others tried to break them out. We got as far as the cells and they told us to go back. They were willing to die just so the Jerries could be satisfied and move on. So we could keep doing our work. They're the real heroes, whatever I do with the rest of this damn war."

Kenneth said, "We can debate that when we have our country back. For now, we can be grateful they left part of your network intact. It was a rare lapse in their intelligence."

Jasper nodded. "You ever think about that?"

Simon said, "About...?"

"Well. You say they flushed out a dozen resistance cells in the same night. How'd they do that?"

Kenneth stopped walking. "Bloody hell."

Jasper looked at them both. "Come on. That had to occur to you at some point."

"We were too busy being focused on what they were planning to worry about how they did it."

"Well, it's worth worrying about, yeah?" Jasper continued walking, and the other two hurried to keep up with him. "Far as I can figure, there are two possibilities. One, they somehow figured out where a dozen cells were located all at once, which implies there's someone who could've given them that information."

Simon shook his head. "No one in our cell. We didn't know where the others were until Kenneth pointed them out. And they didn't know about us as far as I know. And that leaves the other alternative. That they knew where we were located and did nothing until it served their interests. They left us in place until their plan required us to be moved."

Kenneth said, "Any intelligence received by these cells could be compromised. If they knew you were watching..."

"But we ran successful operations. We destroyed a train depot. We interrupted their supply routes."

"Did you?" Jasper said. "Or did you simply do what they expected of you? The last successful operation you ran. How many officers were on-site?"

Simon thought back to the depot, to the two inexperienced officers he and Sandrine killed before sabotaging the tracks. "No. I refuse to believe that information was fed to us. We confirmed it was good. We double-checked the sources. There is no way the Germans could have planted it."

Jasper said, "Of course there is. Where does information come from? Overheard conversations, notes that we read before they reach their final destination. If the Germans knew whose hands the notes would pass through, it would be simple to create a believable fiction. Everyone involved would have no doubt the information could be trusted."

Simon balled his hands into fists. He fought to control his breathing. The thought that Philip's last few months of life had been spent on a ruse was unacceptable. He didn't know how the Germans had pulled off such a massive attack on so many of their cells, but he was now determined to prove they hadn't been wasting their time in Monthyon.

The wolves were in the basement. They had arranged a watch, and now the nights were split up into hour-long shifts. Leopold took the shift before Sandrine's. Despite her offer, Minuet had never arrived to cook dinner for them. Sandrine wasn't terribly worried about the girl's absence. She had been so distraught during their conversation on the road, she was certain Min had decided to give the anxiety a few days to fade before spending time with them again.

Sandrine was awake and stationed in the living room window seat when he returned from his circuit of the property. He came in through the side door and shut it with a very human-like kick of his back foot. Sandrine met him in the kitchen and he rocked his head from side-to-side: nothing amiss. She acknowledged his report with a nod, then opened the basement door for him. The others were already asleep, and he quietly moved down the stairs to join them.

When he was gone she returned to the living room. The moon was three-quarters full and cast enough light for the trees to throw their shadows across the lawn. She was about to turn away when movement caught her eye. She had a mental flash to the night in Monthyon and felt adrenaline surging through her. She remained perfectly still as her eyes swept from one side of the lawn to the other for the source of the disturbance. After a few seconds she saw it, a flicker of shadow near the gate.

Sandrine was already in motion by the time her brain registered something had been seen. She moved on the balls of her feet, loping from the sitting room to the front door in three wide lunges. The door banged off the wall as she launched herself through the opening. She never touched the porch, coming down on the wet grass and feeling it slip under her bare feet as she moved toward the mobile shadow. It was definitely a person, definitely dressed in black, and definitely not supposed to be there. She bared her teeth and fought the urge to transform as she closed the distance between them. She might have been moving on two feet, but the primal side of her mind was in full force as she grabbed the intruder and tackled him to the ground.

"*Merde!*"

The voice was feminine and full of fear, and it was the only reason Sandrine didn't go for a killing blow. Instead they hit the ground on their sides, rolling through the wet grass and snowdrifts until they came to a stop with Sandrine perched on top of her quarry. She squeezed her legs around the other woman's waist and sat up, yanked the knit cap off her head, and confirmed what her ears and nose had already told her about the woman she had just attacked.

"Minuit?!"

The girl stared up at her with terror. Sandrine felt the physical urge to attack boiling in her veins. One fist was gripping the collar of Min's coat hard enough to strain the material, while the other arm was coiled back for a punch. She was trembling with unspent adrenaline, eyes wide open and stinging in the open night air. Her cheeks puffed out with every exhale. She knew that even without the wolf making an appearance Min would see her as something wild, a creature to be feared.

Min reached up and grabbed a handful of Sandrine's hair, pulling her down until their lips met with a crashing kiss. Sandrine growled and thrust her tongue into Min's mouth. She leaned back and used her handful of Min's coat to pull her up as well. She straddled the girl's lap and put both arms around her. She kissed hard enough to bruise the fair girl's mouth, but Min never protested or attempted to calm her assault. Her hands moved to Sandrine's back and she lifted up off the grass to press herself against Sandrine's crotch.

Sandrine broke the kiss and let go of Min's coat, bringing her hand up to her throat. Min gasped in surprised and couldn't draw another breath.

"What do you think you are doing?" she hissed through her teeth.

"You were amped up. Buzzing. I thought you would need an outlet to–"

Sandrine growled. "Not that. What are you doing here? You stupid girl! I should have just taken a rifle and shot at you! I could have blown your stupid head off! You dumb, stupid... careless..." She curled her lip as her fury dissipated. All she could think about was Min's taste and the quick little flickers of her tongue against her lips. She gave up on the scolding and simply kissed Min again, this time taking the younger woman's tongue into her mouth.

When they pulled back again, Min said, "You told me you've spent nights with women. I never have. I've wondered. But I've always been too frightened of making it real. Confronting a woman who may find it disgusting was impossible to me. But since I know... s-since I know you're..."

"I will take you to my bed, Minuit." She cupped Min's face with her palm, extending her thumb to brush it over the girl's lip. "If that is what you came for. It has been a very long time for me, and you are quite lovely." She leaned in and ran her tongue over Min's lips. The girl shuddered in pleasure and tightened her embrace and put her mouth against Sandrine's ear.

"And then you will kill me."

Sandrine recoiled. "What?"

"Make love to me. Make me a woman. And then kill me. Promise."

"I will not."

Min moved her hand to the nape of Sandrine's neck and grabbed a handful of her hair. "Kill me. Fuck me and then kill me in the morning. I am begging you, Sandrine." Her eyes were swimming with tears. She was trembling so violently that tears were shaken free to roll down her face and drip off her jaw. "I beg of you, I have to die."

Sandrine pulled away from Min, violently disentangling them. She shoved Min down onto the grass as she stood up.

"You are ill."

Min grabbed at the shorts Sandrine had put on as pajamas. "No. Please, if you knew, you would understand. I am a demon."

Sandrine yanked Min's hands away. "Go home, Minuit. This is a trying time. You will regret what you are asking me to do. And I will never do it. If you ask me again, I will have you expelled from the resistance. We do not need martyrs." She turned and began walking back toward the house.

"Please! I have to die! I have to die in the next four days! I cannot live through it again."

Sandrine froze in place, one step away from the porch. She lifted her head to the moon, full save for a small sliver of darkness on one side. In four days it would be full. She thought of the secret Min was concealing and everything the girl had said about it, about the shame and self-loathing she had for whatever dark truth she concealed. Suddenly it all made sense. She turned and looked at the weeping girl kneeling in the grass a few feet away from her.

"You are a wolf."

Min's voice caught and she lifted her head slowly. She blinked away her tears and sniffled loudly, hugging herself against the cold. Sandrine stalked back to her.

"Are you? Are you *canidae*?"

"I-I don't kn-know what that is."

"Do you change? Do you become a wolf?"

Min's eyes widened with hope as her brow furrowed with

confusion. The two expressions warred on her face. "H-ho-how did you... how could you possibly guess that?"

Sandrine held out her hand. "Because you have finally found someone who can help you. Come with me. There's something I want to show you inside."

Min swallowed a lump in her throat and put her hand in Sandrine's. She stood up and let herself be led into the house. Sandrine thought about the girl's ignorance of the very word *canidae*. If she reached puberty at thirteen, then she had been changing for at least seven years without knowing what was happening. She felt the deepest sympathy for the girl as she recalled her own teenage transformations. It had been hard enough with *maman* and *papa* to explain everything that was happening. To go through that alone? Minuit had to be much tougher than Sandrine had been giving her credit for.

Min hesitated at the basement door. "You're going to do it, aren't you? You're going to take me down there and kill me."

"No. Be calm. Come." She turned on the light and led Min down the narrow stairs. By the time they reached the bottom landing, Ivonne was standing on all four legs, her head tilted quizzically at the guest Sandrine was bringing them. The other three wolves were also awake, but still lying down with their heads on their paws. Ambrose and Maxime were curled up together.

Sandrine put her hands on Min's shoulders. "Min. I'd like to once again introduce you to the Loupin resistance cell. Ivonne, say hello."

Ivonne twisted and shifted until a naked brunette was standing in front of them. She held out her hand. "Hello, Minuit."

Minuit reached out to take Ivonne's hand. She was shaking again, eyes wide with reverence now, and she exhaled sharply when Ivonne squeezed her hand. She stepped forward and Ivonne smiled before wrapping the girl in a tight embrace. Sandrine stepped forward as well and touched the back of Min's head.

"It's all right. You're home now, pup. You've found your home."

Min sagged in Ivonne's arms and began sobbing again.

CHAPTER TEN

JASPER ASKED them to wait by the curb while he went in and warned his housemates that he was bringing guests in. Once he was out of earshot, Kenneth asked Simon, "Do you think he has a point? About the possibility the Germans knew where you were and fed you information?"

Simon crossed his arms over his chest. "I would say of course not. It's a ridiculous accusation. There is no possibility that Philip and I could have been misled." After a moment he sighed. "But realistically, yes. If the lie is buried deep enough and passes through the hands of enough people who believe it, then anything will start to have the ring of truth. We could have been deceived. But true damage was done. We destroyed the tracks at a train depot. Sandrine and I slaughtered two German soldiers the same night our home was attacked."

Kenneth said, "The same night? You killed two Germans and then... oh. I see."

Simon looked at him.

"You thought you were to blame. You thought the men who attacked your house followed you there from the depot. All this time, you've been punishing yourself for Philip's death."

"The timing..." Simon's face twitched and he quickly looked

away. "We were always careful. We covered our tracks, we checked and re-checked our information. But that night we were hasty. We knew we had to destroy the tracks before another shipment came through, and there was no information about when it would happen. We hurried. And it seemed so easy."

He was afraid Kenneth would try to comfort him, or put a hand on his shoulder. Instead the Brit kept his distance and looked down at the ground.

"I've had my share of failures," Kenneth said. "One of my first missions—"

"I don't need you to regale me with tales of someone you lost." He nodded toward the house. "Jasper is coming back."

The young shoeshine boy had obviously seen that they were deep in conversation and had hung back until they were finished. When Kenneth turned to face the house, Jasper closed the distance in a few long strides. The lights were on in the house and they backlit him with a pale orange glow.

"I've warned them you're coming, so you don't have to worry about anyone shooting when you walk in. We also decided that it's far too late for you to leave, so you're welcome to stay."

Kenneth said, "That won't be necessary. We have methods of traveling undetected at night."

"Foolproof ways? Ways that guarantee you won't be shot dead by a patrol?" Kenneth hesitated. "That's what I thought. I'd be lying if I said we had more than enough room, but we do have space for you to bed down until morning. Even if you could guarantee your way was safe, you've been on the road all day. You must be exhausted. It would also give us a chance to tell you everything we know. Not sure how much that will be."

Kenneth looked to Simon for approval. Simon nodded.

"Thank you, Jasper. That's very kind of you."

He led them inside where a group of resistance members were gathered around the kitchen table. They were a motley group that didn't inspire confidence. Young and wearing threadbare clothes, hair tangled and shaggy, and none of them looking like they could lift a gun let alone shoot it. Jasper introduced them, but Simon was too distracted by his own thoughts to remember any names. He nodded politely to them and thanked them for their hospitality.

"We all have jobs similar to mine. We call ourselves the Invisibles. We shine shoes or beg for coins on the street corners or sit in dark alleys next to fancy restaurants. We don't have to hide because the Germans are going out of their way not to notice us. Because we don't exist to them, we hear everything." He pointed to one of the boys leaning against the kitchen wall. "Tell them what you told me."

The boy straightened his shoulders and faced the strangers. "There is a man... an *Oberst* named Karl Ulrich. He was brought in a few months ago from Egypt. Did you hear about Tobruk?"

Kenneth said, "Devastating loss. Thirty-five thousand Allied troops were forced to surrender, and we handed the Axis Powers a vital port. They're one step away from the Suez."

"Apparently whatever is happening up north is Ulrich's reward for being part of that," the kid said. "Years of service, you know, capped with a big embarrassing victory for Mr. Churchill."

Another resistance member said, "He got here about a month ago. Brought a bunch of friends from Africa with him."

Simon said, "Tanks?"

"Not that we've seen, no," Jasper said. He scanned the room to see if anyone disagreed with his statement. "Mostly trucks. Big trucks, with a lot of construction equipment."

"Construction?" Kenneth said. "They're building something?"

A woman seated at the table ticked off the possibilities with her fingers. "Barracks, a base, a prison, a processing facility. Hell, it could even be an airport. There's plenty of room out here for something of that size."

Simon said, "Whatever it is, we've already lost six months. Whatever they're doing must already be near completion if they're already bringing in someone as big as Ulrich apparently is." He made a mental note to see what he could learn about the German officer. Gilles and Didier were good at abductions. If they got their hands on one of the soldiers heading north, Irene and Anatole could utilize their interrogation skills to find out more. "You've obviously been keeping your eyes and ears open. You've done well."

"There's more."

Jasper motioned to a boy who had been sitting on the floor out of sight. The boy gathered up his notebook and handed it over with charcoal-smudged fingers. Jasper thanked him with a nod before handing the pad over to Simon. The top sheet was a drawing of Simon and Kenneth so realistic it looked like a photograph. Jasper prompted Simon to turn the page. He did, and discovered a handful of portraits done in the same realistic style.

"Don't know who taught him how to do that. He says he just draws the same lines he sees." He shrugged and looked at the boy. "It's handy, though. He's accurate, as you can see, and quick as a bug. Those people you see there are the ones he saw long enough to get a mental image of them. He only did from the neck up, but you can imagine them all in those damn Nazi togs."

"This is very helpful. Thank..." He looked for the boy, but he had vanished again.

Jasper chuckled and patted Simon's arm. "Like I said. We are the Invisibles. Even when we're among friends, we make ourselves disappear. Come. We've all had hard days and I think it's time we got some rest. You can take the book with you when you leave."

"Are you sure?" Kenneth asked.

"We started a record to confirm no one was coming through twice, and that no one who went north was coming back this way. It also served to get a sort of population tally. I don't know how many went by before we started keeping track or how many are moving via other routes, but there are at least forty-five soldiers out there in the middle of nowhere."

"In a time of war, no one would waste that many soldiers standing in a field."

Jasper nodded. "Follow me. I'll show you where you can sleep tonight." He led them out of the kitchen. Simon tucked the book under his arm, nodded his thanks, and followed Kenneth and Jasper down a dark corridor. "It's difficult," Jasper said as he turned on the light in what appeared to be a closet. "We sit here and we count uniforms, we mark down how many faces we see, and we do nothing. We don't fight or try to stop them. We sit on our asses and watch as people we love are taken away, never to be seen again. They stole our country right out from under us, and we shine their boots and give them food that should be going to our families."

Kenneth said, "You're doing the right thing. If you stood up and fought, they would either kill you or take you away. Then we wouldn't have any information. The battle you're fighting is simply more subtle than ours."

Jasper smiled in a way that revealed he didn't believe Kenneth, but he appreciated the effort. "Whatever we can do to help." He gestured at the room. Simon decided it did seem wide enough for two men to lie down, if only just. "Sorry it's not more spacious."

"It's better than wet grass and a rock for a pillow. It'll do fine."

"Okay. Then we'll see you in the morning for breakfast. I'll tell everyone to think long and hard about whether there's anything else you need to know before you leave."

He pointed them toward the bathroom and retrieved pillows and blankets donated from other resistance members before wishing them pleasant dreams. Kenneth pushed his hair out of his face. "I suppose I'll take the north wall, you take the south?"

"Whatever works for you."

Simon tossed down his pillow and stretched out his blanket so he would be in front of the door. Kenneth moved to lay out his bedding against the far wall. Despite Simon's initial misgivings, there was almost enough room between them for another person. If that person was slender and didn't mind laying on her side. Simon propped his pillow against the wall and leaned against it so he could go through the sketchbook.

"What do you think?"

"I think they look like Germans," Simon said. "I think there are far too many of them roaming around in the empty countryside for me to feel comfortable." He flipped to the next page. "*Oberst* Ulrich. The Germans coming out of the Sahara are a hard-scrabble sort. Philip heard some things about them before..." He trailed off. "Before. Their tanks would constantly break down and they can't get new parts because they're made by the Brits. All their food is infested with flies, and that's the food that isn't spoiled by the time it gets to them. I'm extremely concerned that Ulrich is the sort who not only survived that, but he's coming off a victory. It makes him a dangerous adversary now that he's back in a more comfortable climate."

Kenneth was stretched out on the floor next to him, arms behind his head. "This will be a bigger plot than you've ever been part of. Sabotaging train tracks is one thing, but going up against a

German hero and taking out a facility that will apparently house over forty soldiers?"

"Do you doubt we are capable?"

"Not necessarily. I've told you from the beginning that I'm deferring to you on this mission. You know your cell better than I ever could. You know what they're capable of. And right now, I'm asking you a very simple question. Do you think they can handle it? There's no shame in saying they aren't. The more I hear about Ulrich and whatever the Nazis are planning here, the more I fear we're woefully ill-equipped to deal with it. In a perfect world, I would be going back to Paris and demanding three more squadrons and an air strike."

"My pack can handle it," Simon said.

"Are you certain?"

Simon closed the sketchbook and put it on the floor between them. "The mission will be a success no matter what. We'll stop Ulrich and whatever he is planning at all costs."

"Even if your pack doesn't survive?"

"Whatever the cost," Simon reiterated. "Philip gave his life for the cause. The rest of us would do nothing less. Of course we will do everything in our power to ensure we walk away in one piece with no casualties on our side. But if we die, then we die for a just cause. We'll die so others can live. I would have no regrets with a death like that."

Kenneth nodded slowly.

Simon looked up at the chain hanging from the light fixture. "I'm not going to bother with the light. If you want it off, you can stand up and do it."

"I'm fine. I wanted to look through the sketchbook."

"Suit yourself." He rolled onto his side and covered his head with the pillow. He heard Kenneth shift on his blanket and then the shuffle of papers.

He thought about what they'd learned; vague facts and the name of the snake's head: Karl Ulrich. He hadn't just been posturing for the Brit's sake. He was certain every member of the pack felt the same way. He didn't even have to know what the Germans' ultimate goal was. If stopping it came at the cost of their lives, it was a price he would gladly pay. It was what they'd all signed up for when the war began. It was a debt he owed. And when the time came to make good on his promise, he wouldn't shirk from the responsibility.

He closed his eyes listening to the sound of Kenneth flipping pages and drifted off into a dark and dream-filled sleep.

CHAPTER ELEVEN

IN SIMON'S dream, the pack was united once more. They were living in Monthyon and it was springtime. He realized as he walked his subconscious memory of its streets that it was the last place he'd felt at home. They'd left it behind only six months earlier, but already the peaceful little commune seemed like an entirely different life. It was just the pack. More importantly it was him and Philip. They made a home together, a fortress where the wolves closest to them could be safe and plan their sabotages.

When he became aware of his dream, he directed himself to the happiest he had been in the house. He first moved in after discovering Philip and the others using the printing press. Even after their primal fuck in the woods, Simon refused to believe he was truly attracted to another man. He focused his attentions on Irene instead. She was a lean and athletic woman who wore men's clothing, passing as a man in places where she otherwise wouldn't have been granted access. Simon first went to her a few nights after his encounter with Philip. He wanted to prove it had been an aberration, that he was still attracted to women, so he seduced her.

Irene allowed Simon to take her to bed. He was a wild and insatiable lover, and he was willing to go down on her while waiting for his own equipment to recover. He was a damn good lay and she wasn't above taking advantage of it. She told him as much one night as they lay together, his head on her breast as he tried to catch his breath. She knew she was just a distraction for him. He denied it. She kissed his hair and told him she would be there the next time he came calling.

One night he arrived and found she wasn't alone. Philip was sitting on her bed with his back to the door. He wasn't wearing a shirt, and Simon was so distracted by the sight of his muscled shoulders that he almost didn't see Irene. She was kneeling between Philip's legs with her lips around the thick cock rising from the front flap of his trousers. His first instinct - or so he told himself - was to step back through the door and give them privacy. But his own cock had become hard at the sight, and he reached down to adjust it as Irene opened her eyes and saw him.

She crooked her finger for him to come closer. The fact she was there made it acceptable, made it less queer in his eyes, and he was able to justify how much he wanted to join them. He walked into the room and rounded the foot of the bed. Philip realized he was there and watched as Simon sat beside him. They locked eyes and Philip smiled. Simon swallowed and watched Irene's lips and tongue. He could distinctly remember the candlelight glistening off the pink head, the way a line of spit stretched between the shaft and Irene's bottom lip until her stroking fingers broke it.

With her free hand, Irene unfastened Simon's trousers and took his cock out. He swelled in her hand, his thigh pressing against Philip's. She let Philip fall from her mouth and leaned to the side, circling the head of Simon's cock before taking it into her mouth as well. He closed his eyes and ran one hand through the hair she kept short and shaggy to help with her disguise as a man. She alternated between the men, stroking one while sucking the other.

After a few minutes of keeping both men on the edge of orgasm, Irene leaned back. Her mouth was shining. "I'm getting seasick leaning back and forth. Stand up. Here."

Simon and Philip stood on either side of her, facing each other. Irene gripped them both and pulled them closer, grunting with desire as their cocks lined up in front of her mouth. Her tongue danced from one to the other and she used her fingers to keep them from drifting apart. Simon throbbed and twitched against the smooth, silky skin of the other man's cock. His face was red as he looked down at Irene's harsh, masculine features, her pink tongue curling around his shaft before sliding over to Philip's. Simon exhaled at the sight of his cock squeezed tight against Philip's thicker, darker penis. Simon's body was darker and thickly-haired. Philip's was lean and muscled, the hair neatly trimmed to show off his pinker skin.

"Touch each other for me," Irene said. It was the "for me" that made Simon's hand move to Philip's balls. If he'd let himself believe it was something he wanted to do, he never would have found the courage. But he reached between Philip's legs and squeezed the heavy sack. Philip exhaled sharply and whispered something under his breath.

"Louder," Irene scolded.

"Simon," Philip said. "That feels good."

Simon's face burned hotter. Irene closed her lips around Simon's cock and pulled him into her mouth, sucking and moaning around his length. She let him thrust into her mouth a few times, and then dropped him to let Philip do the same. It was their turn to move, guiding their cocks to her and letting her decide whether or not to switch. After a few seconds she took the head of both cocks into her mouth and they thrust together.

Philip was watching Simon carefully and reached out to smooth his hand over the curve of Simon's ass. Simon arched his back and told himself it was so he could push deeper into Irene's mouth, but in actuality he wanted to feel the hard length of Philip's cock brushing against his. He put his hand on the back of Philip's head and drew him closer. Philip dug his fingers into Simon's ass, and then they were kissing.

It felt so good to finally give in to the urge that Simon barely noticed the hand wrapped around his cock was too large and rough to be female. He didn't care that Irene stopped sucking him, assuming that she was just focusing on Philip. But then he felt her fingers on his wrist. When she guided him to take Philip's cock in his hand, his fingers closed around it automatically. Philip tightened his grip and began stroking, and Simon did the same.

Irene became a ghost, her hands gliding over their bodies as she shed their clothes. Simon leaned forward to feel Philip's chest against his, and Philip moaned into his mouth as Simon's thumb brushed over the head of his cock. Irene broke their kiss, begging Simon to kiss her before she kissed Philip's lips. She stepped away, and the men fell against each other again. Soon the need to come was unbearable, and Simon reached for her with his free hand. His fingers closed on empty air.

He broke the kiss and looked around the suddenly empty room. "Irene...?"

"She left." Philip's voice was low and rumbling.

Simon knew he needed release, and suddenly he had only one option. The choice clicked in his brain, not really a choice at all but a sudden freedom to do what he wanted to do in the first place. He shoved Philip onto the bed and climbed on top of him, growling as he lifted the other man's legs onto his thighs. Philip watched him, stroking his cock as Simon positioned himself against Philip's ass. Both of them were breathing heavily. Looking down at himself, Simon saw sweat shining through the hair on his chest and stomach. His face was burning as he rubbed himself against the spot beneath Philip's balls.

Without warning, Philip reached down and grabbed Simon's cock. The grip was almost unbearable, and Simon had to fight the urge to spill all over Philip's hand.

"Say it. Say what you want."

"Let go of me."

"You have to say it this time, Simon."

He bared his teeth. "I could walk away."

"So do it."

Simon whimpered and leaned forward. Their faces were inches apart; he felt the warmth washing off of Philip's face.

"I want to fuck you."

"Say it."

"I want..." He shoved Philip's hand away and repositioned himself. "To fuck you."

Philip dropped back onto the mattress with a cry of pleasure, reaching out to grab Simon's arms to pull him down as well. Simon gripped the sheets on either side of Philip's head, his knee digging into the edge of the mattress as he began to thrust. Philip moved his hand between their bodies to stroke himself, arching his back as

Simon kissed his chin and jaw, pushing into him so hard that the bed's entire frame moved with the force of it.

Later they would discover Irene was still in the room. She'd only retreated to the corner so she could step in if either man rebelled at the idea of what she was doing. She told them that they'd been gorgeous together, that she'd made herself come by the time Simon finally climaxed inside of Philip with an explosive cry. When Philip rolled them and settled on top of Simon, both men were moving with the slow and measured movements of exhaustion. Their sex was slower the second time because it had to be, and Simon reached back to guide Philip's thrusts as he pressed his own erection into the tangled sheets underneath his body.

Eventually they fell asleep in each other's arms. When Simon woke the next morning, he was no longer interested in fighting what he felt for his pack leader. His memories mixed with conscious thought as he woke up. A lifetime of waking up in unusual places had taught him to know his surroundings, so he didn't have the momentary panic he'd heard other people experienced in situations like these. He knew he was on the floor of a miniscule room in Jasper's home. He knew that it was sometime between three and four in the morning. And he knew the body next to him was Kenneth Mackay.

He heard the rustling of cloth before his eyes adjusted well enough for him to see the shape of his roommate. Kenneth was lying under his blankets, the leg closest to Simon bent at the knee to offer a modicum of privacy. But Simon could hear his heavy breathing, smelled the reek of desire that filled the small space, and knew precisely what the Brit was doing. He could feel a wet spot in his own underwear, so he also knew that he must have prompted Kenneth's actions.

Kenneth grunted softly and thrust his hips. Simon felt himself stir despite his recent orgasm. He thought about closing the distance between them, lifting up Kenneth's blanket, giving him a final act he wouldn't forget. But he stopped himself before he moved. He simply touched himself through his clothes, idly stroking until his cock was standing at attention. He closed his fist around the material and closed his eyes as he squeezed and moved his hips.

In the moments before orgasm, Kenneth grunted a name that

Simon couldn't quite make out. He exhaled and sighed when he was finished, and he stretched his leg out until both feet were flat against the wall. The blankets shifted again as he rolled onto his side.

"I hope you enjoyed the show. After all, you inspired it."

"Still enjoying it," Simon said.

Kenneth said, "Ah. You were quite loud. Must have been quite a dream."

"Memory." He was breathing hard through his nose. "The first man I ever loved. I was fucking him. And then he was fucking me."

Kenneth said, "Was he gentle with you?"

"Only when I wanted him to be."

Kenneth chuckled and lay flat again. Simon put his hand into his pants, his palm cold against the overheated skin of his erection. He came on his palm and fingers, twitching with the release, and then pulled his hand free. He held the hand out from under the blankets. Kenneth drew in a slow, deep breath and let it out even slower. The room reeked of sweat and sex, and Simon knew they were just six inches away from doing something they would probably regret. Even if the time was right, they couldn't risk Jasper or anyone from his cell overhearing. Someone could believe the Nazis were evil but agree with them on homosexuality being deviant behavior. They couldn't risk alienating a potential source of good information.

Simon rearranged the pillow under his head. It was bad enough he and Philip had risked their cell by adding personal feelings to the mix. It wasn't a mistake he was going to repeat, especially not with a temporary associate like Kenneth Mackay.

Chapter Twelve

"My parents found me in a river when I was a baby."

Minuit was sitting in the living room surrounded by women of the pack. Irene and Ivonne were sitting on either side of her. Sandrine was standing in front of her and to one side, so the girl could see that her escape route wasn't being blocked. The door was in plain view and completely open to her if she chose to leave. Ivonne and Irene had put on blouses but their legs were bare, and Min's eyes kept drifting to their bare, muddy feet as if they were still wolf paws. She had fallen silent again.

"You don't have to tell us anything you don't want to," Ivonne said.

"I want to. God, I want to." She closed her eyes. Her fingers were linked together, and she brought them up to her lips. "I've held this in so long, it feels good to say it. But it's also hard to find the words to say it. Am I making sense?"

Sandrine nodded.

"My father found me in a sack. He thought someone was trying to drown kittens, so he fished the bag out and got a baby instead. My mother couldn't have children, so they thought God was giving them a miracle. If I had been a boy they would have called me Moses." She smiled weakly and flexed her fingers. "When I was twelve, it happened for the first time. I woke up with such horrible cramps. My mother had warned me of becoming a woman, so I thought that was what it was. But then I... my hands were... a-and my f-face. I stayed in my room. My parents had no idea. I was myself when morning came. I tried to ask my parents about it, but they were completely clueless. My father took me to the library because he thought I had heard fairy tales. He wanted me to read them from the source. That's how I found out what I am. Werewolf."

"*Canidae.*"

She looked at Irene. "I didn't know there was a word for it. I didn't know there was anyone else like me outside of storybooks." She wiped at her eyes and sniffled. "I thought I was possessed by a demon. That was why my parents tried to kill me after I was born. They knew I was wrong."

Sandrine said, "You're not wrong. You're one of us."

"You're all... the entire cell?"

Ivonne nodded. "Philip found us all. He made us into a team. But we grew up with *canidae* parents who told us what we are, how to survive as a wolf. You weren't so fortunate. When you told Sandrine you were going to change in four days, that's from the stories. Right?"

"The full moon," Min said.

"Fables," Irene said. "We can change whenever we wish, as you saw earlier. The full moon legend is just because we're easier to see by the light of a full moon. The rest of the month there are plenty of shadows to hide in. Our parents taught us the difference between myth and truth. They also taught us how to coexist with our wolves. I can't imagine the hell you've been going through. How old are you? Twenty-two?"

"Twenty-four."

"A full decade." Ivonne said. "Horrific. I can't even imagine what you've been through, you poor thing. Stay here with us tonight. In the morning we can discuss this further, show you a few rudimentary tricks to help you through the transformation. It is not a horrifying thing and you are not a demon. You are not a monster. You are a miracle."

"Thank you all," Min said, though she was looking at Sandrine. "I would like to spend the night in Sandrine's room, if that's all right with her."

Sandrine tensed, but her anxiety became irritation when she saw Irene and Ivonne exchanging a look of amusement.

"I don't think that would be wise. The couch will do just fine."

"But~"

"We all need our rest," Sandrine said. "Irene, you and Ivonne can go back downstairs. We'll brief the others in the morning."

Irene stopped hiding her amusement. "If you're certain, Sandrine."

"Go."

They shuffled off and Sandrine glared at their backs. When she heard the basement door close, she returned her gaze to the girl.

"Your day tomorrow will be bigger than any of ours. Get plenty of rest."

"I think I've been resting long enough."

Sandrine rolled her eyes. "Good night, Minuit." She walked away without looking back; she didn't want to give the girl any indication she was second-guessing herself. And even though she didn't look, she could feel Min's eyes on her back the entire walk through the kitchen. She returned to the master bedroom upstairs, which she was sharing with Amorette, Dorsey, and Gilles. The door was open, and she could feel the others inside. It was more than smelling them; it was an innate awareness that they were nearby. She craved that closeness, even if she would never say it out loud. The members of her pack would never need her to say it to know it was true.

She was on the threshold before she heard a footstep on the stairs behind her. Min stopped at the head of the stairs when Sandrine looked at her, one hand resting on the banister as she hesitated. After a few seconds of silence she took the next step and joined Sandrine on the landing. She moved closer and Sandrine stepped away from the bedroom to meet her in the middle. Min wet her lips to speak but Sandrine put a finger against her mouth to stop her. She could see everything that needed to be said in the girl's expression.

After years of feeling like a freakish monster, Min found a place where she was normal. She found people who not only accepted her for what she was, they were like her as well. That was frightening and liberating at the same time. She suddenly had every answer she'd ever wanted laid out in front of her waiting to be given. She would finally understand the side of her she always considered horrific. For the first time in her life she had a place where she could be comforted. A home.

Min's expression shifted slightly. Sandrine knew that she was reading her face as well, and she hoped the girl was wise enough to decipher it properly. She wanted Min to know she was welcomed in the house and, if she wanted, she would be welcome in the pack as well. The words carried too much weight to say aloud so early in their acquaintance with each other, but she meant them just the same. Wolves needed a pack, and Min had gone long enough by herself.

They stood silently for a few moments before Min opened her mouth and let Sandrine's finger fall onto her tongue. She held eye contact as she sucked it down to the first knuckle and stepped closer to the older woman. Sandrine didn't look away but she took a step backward. Her free hand went around Min's waist and she spun, pinning the girl against the wall. She added a second finger and Min sucked it eagerly, her eyes finally closing as she put her hands on Sandrine's waist.

Sandrine pulled her fingers from Min's mouth and ran the side of her hand down the girl's body. She cut a line between her breasts, over her stomach, and down to her belt. She was wearing a skirt. Sandrine lifted the material and Min bit her lip, the soles of her shoes scraping on the floor when she moved them further apart.

"Have you ever been touched before?"

"No."

"Do you want me to touch you now?"

Min gave a quiet squeak before she said, "Yes."

Sandrine pressed her hand against Min's crotch, stroking her wet fingers against the crotch of her underwear. Min bit off a yelp of surprised and clapped a hand over her mouth. She squeezed her eyes shut and then snapped them open to stare at Sandrine. One finger twisted the cotton out of the way and Sandrine pressed her knuckle against the virgin flesh, rocking her wrist forward and back until she felt moisture building. She leaned forward and put her lips against Min's neck. She ran the flat of her tongue from the collar to the line of hair behind Min's ear, inhaling deeply to pick up every fragrance. Sweat overwhelmed soap and set off primal triggers in Sandrine's mind.

"Do you smell me, Minuit?"

"I..."

She put her free hand on the back of Min's head and brought it forcefully down onto her shoulder. Min nuzzled her and then took a breath. "Oh," she whispered, sniffing again and this time parting her lips. "Oh, Sandrine. You smell... you smell so good..." She dragged her teeth along Sandrine's throat. Sandrine responded by tilting her head back and gazing at the ceiling. She had both fingers inside of Min now, and Min was thrusting against the meaty part of her hand.

In the bedroom, bodies shifted against bedclothes. She could feel their interest, their want, but she didn't tell Min. She wasn't sure if it would make the girl too self-conscious so she just kept her silence and continued to thrust her hand forward. Min stretched away from her, thumped her head against the wall, and released a choked-off cry as she came. Her face contorted. For the briefest of moments Sandrine thought Min was going to transform mid-orgasm. She stretched her mouth wide and jutted her chin forward. The skin around her eyes seemed to darken, but that might have just been the shadows playing tricks on Sandrine's eyes. The girl was fighting the change.

"Show me your wolf," Sandrine growled. "You can slip right into the shift after you come. Show me your wolf." She stepped back and began yanking Min's clothes off, tossing each item aside until the girl stood naked in front of her. She retreated to the other side of the hall and Min fell forward. Her scream of pain turned into a howl as she arched her back.

Sandrine unfastened her own pants and pushed her hand between her legs, touching herself as she watched Min change. It was over in a matter of seconds, but Sandrine was so aroused that she finished while Min was still shaking her fur. She pulled her hand free and knelt in front of the wolf. Min's eyes, wide and blue and full of her human intelligence stared back. She was obviously terrified, but Sandrine pressed a kiss to her sloping forehead and then to the side of her snout.

"You are safe now. You are among your family." She brushed her hand over the top of Min's head and stood up. She gestured for Min to follow her into the master bedroom. There was a large bed where Gilles and Amorette had been sleeping with Dorsey in the middle. They were up now, and Dorsey had transformed into her wolf before dropping onto the floor and approaching Min. Gilles and Amorette were sitting up on the bed, nude and entangled with sheets but not so well that Gilles' erection was hidden. They were both heavily aroused by what they had just overheard, as well as the smell of sex emanating from the new arrivals.

Dorsey walked around Min, who stood extremely still during the examination. When they were face to face, Dorsey opened her jaw wide and closed it over Min's muzzle. Sandrine smiled and bent down to smooth her hand over Min's flank so she wouldn't be alarmed. Min looked back at her, and Sandrine could read the request in her eyes. She nodded and stood up, shed her clothes, and shifted into her wolf.

Min approached and sniffed her, as if confirming it was really Sandrine. They rubbed their snouts together. Sandrine flicked her tongue out across Min's mouth, then nudged her closer to the bed. Dorsey hopped up onto the mattress. Sandrine nudged Min to follow her before joining the other four wolves on the bed. Dorsey lay across Gilles' lap, her haunches in Amorette's, and Min stretched out at their feet. Sandrine settled in beside her and rested her head on Min's shoulders.

In the morning Min would get the official welcome, and her induction to the pack would have to wait until Simon returned. But for the time being she seemed to be fitting in extremely well. Sandrine listened to the young wolf's breathing become steadier until the rhythm of it lulled her into a deep and dreamless sleep.

CHAPTER THIRTEEN

MIN WAS far less forward in the morning, having grown self-aware after her boldness. The whole pack stepped forward to make her feel welcome. Ivonne drew her a bath, a luxury no one else allowed themselves. Gilles offered to cook whatever she wanted for breakfast - his only limitation being what was in the pantry.

Once everyone was in human form, they greeted her properly. The girl seemed overwhelmed by the sudden acceptance of her long-hidden secret. Sandrine didn't want to add to the overstimulation and left the girl to bond with her new family. She went into the living room to look at her map. Information from all over the north of France had resulted in a latticework of strings, all of them converging in the same general area. She put her finger in the nexus of her web to spread it wide enough to see the part of the map underneath it.

Min carried the scent of buttered bread and the chicory they were using as a substitute for coffee. "Is that the map?"

Sandrine nodded and withdrew her finger. She turned around to accept the coffee Min was offering her. She was surprised to see Min was only wearing an unbuttoned shirt over a pair of underwear that didn't belong to her.

"Whose clothes are you wearing?"

"Gilles. He woke me up this morning." Her cheeks flushed pink. "He said if there was anything I needed, I could come to him."

Sandrine stepped around Min and went into the kitchen. Gilles was at the stove and glanced back when he heard her coming.

"Ah, hello. The next batch of biscuits is nearly ready. It's not quite~"

She cut him off by grabbing his throat and shoving him across the room, only stopped when his head bounced off the yellow flowers of the wallpaper. She stepped in front of him with her spine stretched, standing on her toes, her entire body poised for an attack. When she spoke, spittle flew from her lips and dotted his face.

"Leave her be. You do not touch that girl. You do not soil her with your filth, Gilles."

"I don't..."

She rapped his head against the wall again.

"All right. All right. I was just being friendly."

Sandrine let him drop and stepped back.

He rubbed his throat and glared at her. "Are you laying claim to her? Because you're going to have to if you want her to yourself."

She knew the unspoken rule in the pack was that every relationship was open unless explicitly stated. Simon and Phillip had been one such example of exclusivity, but even they occasionally went to bed with other members of the pack. If she wanted to declare Min for herself, she would have to accept the commitment for what it was.

"She's not for me. She's not for anyone. Am I making myself clear?"

He straightened and rocked his head from side to side. "More than you know, Sandrine. You are transparent."

She ignored the implication of his words and turned her back on him. When she returned to the living room, Min was examining the map. Sandrine stopped behind her, and Min touched the spot where the strings converged.

"This isn't empty."

"It certainly looks that way on the map."

"It's not a good map. I've seen it myself. There is a lot of wide open space, yes, but there is also a large building on the river. Near these train tracks." She moved the strings so Sandrine could see.

"Look, this field? It's not empty. The building has been abandoned for at least a decade, but it's surrounded by a huge stone wall with iron gates."

Sandrine felt it in her bones that this was the place they had been looking for. Every German transport that traveled north had been converging in this area, and now there was a mysterious empty building for them to congregate? That had to be the place they were going.

She put her hand on Min's shoulder. "We have to go investigate this immediately. Go put some clothes on. You can come with us."

"Really?"

"It's your revelation. You deserve to see it through. Besides, you're the only one who knows where this building is. We need you there."

"I'll send a message to Sylvester to let him know where we're going. And... thank you."

"Don't thank me. You're part of the pack now. You're only fulfilling your responsibility."

Min said, "Yes, ma~"

"Don't you dare call me ma'am. Just go."

Min smiled and hurried upstairs. Sandrine looked at the map again and found Chauny, the commune where Simon and Kenneth were headed as of their last report. She wanted to meet up with them on the road, if at all possible, and continue the rest of the way with them. She had a good feeling about Min's information. The Nazis would eagerly take over such a gloriously convenient base of operations. Now all that remained was finding out what they were doing there and stopping them.

"For Philip," she whispered. She thumped her knuckle against the wall and went to gather some of Gilles' biscuits for the road.

They set out a few minutes before eight-thirty. Sandrine and Leopold's cover story was that they were married and looking for work. Min was Leopold's younger sister, and Didier was the grandfather of the group. Sandrine smiled when she saw Didier's moth-eaten sweater and the cane Sylvester insisted he carry. His reasoning was that it would invite the Germans to underestimate him while also providing him with a weapon if necessary. But no matter how practical the prop was, it definitely made Didier look a good decade older than he was.

Didier caught Sandrine's smile. "Feh. You'll be old too, one day. And then what will your role be? Crone? I'm betting crone."

She tweaked the brim of his cap, pulled it off his head, and pushed it down on hers. "As you say, Grandpapa. Come along."

Sylvester had loaned them a car for the trip. Sandrine initially refused, but speed would be their friend. They needed to reach Chauny before Simon and Kenneth left. Then it would be just a quick jaunt from there to the porcelain factory. They piled into the car - Sandrine sitting beside Leopold as he drove, with Min and Didier in the back. Irene was also with them in her wolf form. What was a family without their loyal mutt? The pack members remaining at the house wished them luck, then went back inside before they were spotted by a suspicious neighbor.

Min told them that Sylvester and the others were extremely proud of her, and that her friend Alain had even given her his trench knife, a six-inch blade with a steel crossbar and a walnut handle. The sheath was in her boot. Sandrine twisted in her seat to look at the girl. She was sitting serenely on the passenger side of the car, Irene's wolf lying between her and Didier. Min looked calm and relaxed despite the danger they were heading into.

"You sure you're prepared for this?"

"One hundred percent," Min said without hesitation. "I've been eager to do more than hide and wait for an opportunity to strike. But more than that..." She reached up and ran her hand over Irene's head. "I am finally with my pack. I am home. Whatever awaits us at the factory, if it means nothing or certain death, I am finally at peace with who I am. I am a wolf. And I am homosexual." She blinked rapidly and gently rubbed Irene's ear. "I am ready to fight to defend this. To defend us."

Sandrine nodded and faced forward again. They had a new map provided to them by Urbain, and he'd embellished it with a few red-marked areas to avoid at all costs. A straightforward drive would take them ninety minutes, but the safe path had them reaching Chauny in just about double that time. Sandrine didn't mind the delay. It was still faster than they could have gone on foot, and using the side roads made it more likely they would cross paths with their allies. She played navigator to Leopold, telling him which side roads to take and when, but otherwise she watched the fields roll by out the window.

"What were you? Before?"

Sandrine had been almost hypnotized by the green trees lined up on the horizon. She assumed Min had been talking to someone else but, when no one answered, she looked at the girl over her shoulder. "What? Before when?"

"Before the war broke out."

Sandrine grunted and looked out the window again.

Leopold said, "Sandrine doesn't like discussing that. The past is the past, and it should stay there. She prefers to focus on the present. Me? I was an unemployed cement mason. I had my own business but had to shut it down. Not enough work. I was actually glad when I heard war was coming." He drummed his fingers on the steering wheel. "I'd rather be unemployed, all things considered."

"What's important is now," Sandrine said. "This is what we do now."

They drove in silence for a few more kilometers before Min spoke again. "I only ask because I... I was a student. I graduated from school and I was still living with my parents. I was helping them at their shop while I tried to figure out what to do with my life. Then I was going to wait until after the war. And now..." She stroked Irene's back. "This is what I do. This is the only life I've known. I sometimes worry that when it's over, I won't know what to do with myself."

Didier said, "We'll all find our way. It might take time, but we'll find our way."

Sandrine said nothing. All the times she'd been shot at, stabbed, beaten up, and chased, she had long ago decided she would die in the war. It wasn't that she pursued death. She merely accepted it was close by and didn't waste time or energy trying to outsmart it. Thousands of people had died and thousands more would die before the conflict was over. It was pure egotism to think she would make it through intact. That was why she didn't like to think about the past. That version of her was dead. She would never get to go back to it. What was the purpose of longing?

On a stretch of empty road outside of Chauny, Sandrine told Leopold to pull over. A strip of untended grass ran between the road and the trees, and they knew their friends would've had to come this way on their return trip to Meldeuses. Didier opened the door and Irene clambered out over his lap. He grunted and cursed at her to be careful where she put her feet next time, but she ignored him as she sprinted out across the field with her snout to the ground. She moved in a wide arc before she lifted her head and yipped, tossing her head toward the commune. A second later she was loping in that direction.

"Looks like Simon and Kenneth haven't left town yet," Sandrine said.

Leopold started the car and followed Irene. Outside of the commune, the road had been bordered by trees. Once across the bridge the trees fell back and were replaced by elegant stone walls. Irene stood out more than Sandrine liked, but there was no one to take notice of her as she ran at the base of one wall. Leopold drove slowly to give their friend time to follow a scent, braking now and again as Irene turned in a circle and looked for anything familiar. She would put her nose to the ground, lift her head to scent the air, and then continue jogging.

"Someone is going to take notice of this," Didier said.

Sandrine said, "Germans sleep until noon. No one else will say anything."

"This town could be loyal to the Nazis," Didier grunted. "They may say something just to get in good with their new overlords."

"Then we will silence them," Sandrine said.

They were passing the train depot when Irene suddenly cut across the road. Leopold stood on the brake to keep from hitting her, and they all watched as she ran across the platform. Simon and Kenneth were standing next to the shoeshine stand wearing borrowed clothes and flanking a young man with a weak attempt at a beard. Kenneth saw Irene first and nudged Simon. Leopold stopped the car. Sandrine and Min got out, leaving the men behind so they made less of a spectacle.

Simon had crouched down to scratch the top of Irene's head like she was a dog. The message was received loud and clear: whoever their companion was, he didn't know about *canidae*. He looked up when Sandrine reached him.

"We were just about to head back. Sandrine, this is Jasper. Jasper, Sandrine and Minuit."

Sandrine nodded politely to the young man. "I hope your visit here was fruitful."

Simon said, "We can discuss what we learned later. You wouldn't be here if you didn't have news of your own. What have you found?"

"Perhaps the location of our adversary, whoever it may turn out to be."

Kenneth said, "We may have learned his name. Karl Ulrich."

Sandrine's arms tingled with gooseflesh. There was no evidence either of their discoveries would be fruitful, but she could feel the potential breakthrough was in their grasp.

Jasper cleared his throat. "If you know what rat hole Ulrich has crawled into, I can lend assistance wherever you need it. Men, weapons, food. Whatever."

"I'm certain we'll make good on that offer, Jasper. Thank you."

Sandrine eyed the newcomer warily, but both Simon and Kenneth seemed to trust him. "What do you know of an old porcelain factory just south of here?"

Jasper said, "Not much. It's been closed since before I was born."

Kenneth said, "Porcelain factory?" His entire body was rigid with tension, his eyes almost wild as he stared at Sandrine. "What porcelain factory?"

Sandrine met his gaze. "We received reports from all the agents we sent out. They told us where they saw the Germans heading, and I mapped it out. Min says the lines all converge on a space that looks clear on the map but actually houses a porcelain factory. It would be large enough to house the number of soldiers we've heard about."

"More than that," Kenneth whispered harshly. "Christ, no." He turned around and pushed his hands through his hair as he began to pace. Sandrine and Simon were very aware of the commuters milling about on the platform, but the British officer didn't seem to care that he was causing a scene.

Simon said, "Have you heard of this place before?"

"What?" Kenneth asked, too distracted by his own thoughts to hear what he'd been asked.

"Have you heard of this porcelain factory before?"

Kenneth shook his head. "No. But if I'm correct, we will all have heard about it by war's end." He was breathing heavily. "There are holding facilities near here. Prisons without the luxury of due process. Compounds where undesirables are herded like cattle while they await transport to one hellish final destination or another."

"Concentration camps," Jasper said, spitting the words as if they left ashes on his tongue.

Kenneth nodded. "These abominations were built to hold seven hundred people, but at last report some are holding seven *thousand*. They simply can't risk transporting so many prisoners to Buchenwald or Ravensbrueck. People are dying waiting to be shipped off to be killed." He put his hands over his face. Sandrine noticed his hands were shaking. "Ulrich must be looking for a way to cut down on the population in the processing center."

"So he's building another prison?" Min said.

"No." Kenneth closed his eyes. "They're building a new concentration camp."

CHAPTER FOURTEEN

THE GROUP remained on the platform much longer than they should have. Patrols were passing by, and the last driver had slowed down to examine the bunch before continuing on. Didier finally left the car and suggested they take themselves somewhere less conspicuous. Simon's mind was reeling with the information he'd just received from Sandrine. And Kenneth's theory about what was happening at the porcelain factory was enough to make his stomach twist in knots. He could only think about the faceless Nazi who was apparently running the mission. Ulrich, a cypher in a corpse-gray uniform, a killer who hid behind his orders.

Once they were all squeezed into the car, Leopold drove them back to Jasper's home. Kenneth used the drive to explain the information they'd put together.

Didier grunted and looked out the window. "And how exactly are we supposed to stop them from building one of those godforsaken camps? Do you know how many Jerries have to be buzzing around that place, even if it's not operational yet? And if it is running, we've got the prisoners to worry about. We can't just bomb it back to Hell with innocent people still inside. So you're talking about... what? Just storming in, killing everyone with a skull on their hat, then unlocking all the doors? Where are we going to go with a hundred escaped prisoners?"

Kenneth said, "The camp can't be operational yet."

"It most certainly can," Jasper argued. "It's been six months since they ran you out of Monthyon. They've had all that time to get it ready. And if the other facilities are as overcrowded as we've heard they are, the Germans will jump on the opportunity to spread out their undesirables."

Simon had been staring intently at the floorboards. "It doesn't matter. If there are a hundred prisoners, we will free them all. If there are a hundred guards, then we'll murder every last one of them. We cannot allow another of these charnel houses to become active."

Leopold said, "I concur."

Min cleared her throat. "I might be the youngest member of our cell back in Meldeuses, but I think I can guess they would all agree. We've been wasting our time hiding and having secret meetings. We've been talking about what we would do if granted the opportunity. The opportunity has arisen. Even if the odds are impossibly high, and even if we're assured death, then we'll die for a worthy cause. A few might back out and refuse to help, but the majority of my cell will back you up."

Kenneth said, "So our numbers are greater than we hoped, but we're still going up against a small army." He looked at Simon. "Of course, three different groups coming together. Complications could definitely arise."

Simon knew exactly what Kenneth was trying to say; Min and Jasper's groups weren't savvy to the existence of *canidae*. If it was truly a combined effort, they would either have to keep their most powerful secret weapon in check or find a way to surreptitiously use their wolves without making their new allies suspicious. Sneaking away to make plans the other groups weren't privy to? Simon knew exactly how he would react if anyone from Jasper or Min's outfits did that.

"We'll work out the finer details later," Simon said. "For now we need to regroup. Didier, you will remain here in Chauny with Jasper's group. Fill them in about what's happening. Leopold, you and Irene go back to Meldeuses. We'll need everyone coming up here to lend a hand, regardless of how suspicious such a large migration will look."

Jasper said, "Who is Irene?"

Simon looked at Irene, who was giving him the most reproachful look she was capable of in her wolf form. "Sorry. I meant Sandrine. Although on second thought, I want her with us."

"Where will we be going?" Kenneth said.

"You and I, along with Sandrine, will go investigate the porcelain factory. We need hard facts and not just speculation."

"How will your friend get back to Meldeuses if you're using the car to investigate this lead?" Kenneth started to answer, but Jasper cut him off. "No. We have a car you can borrow. And we have weapons. Rations, too. Take whatever you need from the house."

Kenneth said, "It's much appreciated, Jasper."

"You're the ones doing the real work. We're just providing the pastries and a few bullets."

"If the worst comes to pass, we're going to need more than that," Simon said. "We're going to need bodies to shoot those bullets. And maybe catch a few in return."

Jasper said, "You'll have them, sir."

Simon rested his chin on his fist and gazed out the window. He didn't doubt the dedication of their new friends. He knew Jasper was being sincere in his dedication to the cause. It was, in fact, that dedication making him wary. The group from Meldeuses were all adults, some of them gray and wrinkled. But Jasper's people were children. Teenagers whose elders were those capable of growing facial hair. When he thought about them throwing in their lot to follow him into battle, he wondered how he would ever live with himself after the war ended. If he cost these boys and girls their lives, how was he any better than Hitler ordering German boys to the slaughter?

He wondered if Philip had ever felt the same apprehension. Simon was older than Jasper was when he joined the resistance, but Philip must have thought him so much younger. More innocent and untainted by the horrors of battle.

He'd followed Kenneth's lead this far out of a desire to honor Philip's memory and get vengeance for his death. Now he couldn't help but worry that in doing so, he would become somebody Philip wouldn't have respected.

The car rolled to a stop in front of the house where he and Kenneth spent the night. "We're here," Leopold said. "Now what?"

Simon opened the door, casting aside his doubts so he could act decisively. If not for his sake, then for everyone else's. "Now you go back and get the rest of our people. We have a mission to complete."

As they went into the house to gather supplies, there was a moment when Simon and Sandrine were alone outside. "Minuit is a necessary component on the mission, but she's also a liability. If the need arises for us to use the wolves, we may have to incapacitate her. I know you have a soft spot for her~"

"I have no such thing," Sandrine snapped, a bit too angrily and far too quickly. "Besides, it's not an issue. Remember I said she had a secret? She's one of us."

Simon stopped on the threshold. "Impossible."

"She's one of us," Sandrine said. "She spent last night with the pack."

"Unbelievable," Simon said. "Well, I suppose that makes things much easier, then. Everyone going to this factory will be a wolf. No need for subterfuge."

Sandrine nodded. "And the need will arise. I looked at the maps on our way up here. It's located just south of Saint-Pierre-Aigle. It's a blessing and a curse, really. Lots of heavy woods, but also wide open spaces. They would see anyone coming from miles away if we tried to approach in human form. As wolves, we stand a chance. A small chance, but better than nothing."

"Agreed." They went into the house and rejoined the others.

Jasper made good on his promise. Any weapons they found were handed over without question, and he sent one of the silently hovering members of his cell into the back of the house to gather whatever they could spare from the pantry. Kenneth protested, saying they would only be gone a few days at most, and said they would only take enough for two meals per person.

"We probably couldn't carry much more than that anyway."

"If you're certain," Jasper said. "If you change your mind, you know where to get more. No need to travel all the way back to where you're settled now."

"Much obliged," Kenneth said.

Jasper shrugged. "If we can't help you with the actual mission, we'll be damn certain you'll be prepared for it. We can skip a meal or two, but you need to keep your strength up."

The car Jasper had promised they could borrow was hidden in the barn. Leopold gassed it up and departed for Meldeuses with Irene. Kenneth helped Simon load their things into the other car while Sandrine and Min examined the map for the best route to take. It was just past lunchtime when they departed Chauny and headed south. Simon twisted in his seat and inhaled deeply.

"You don't smell like a wolf."

"She's not like us. Her parents abandoned her in the woods, and she grew up thinking she was possessed by a demon. She only changed when she absolutely had to, during the night of the full moon."

Kenneth said, "The girl is a *canidae?*"

"We discovered the truth after you left for Chauny," Sandrine said.

"Amazing."

Min shifted uncomfortably in her seat. She pulled her hands up into the sleeves of her jacket and pushed them under her thighs. "It's amazing that we've found each other. I thought I was the only one in the whole world, and now I find an entire pack."

"Yes, amazing," Kenneth repeated.

Simon looked at him, noting the harsh line of his jaw. "What?"

"Nothing. I would prefer not to discuss it here."

"By all means," Sandrine said, "discuss it here."

He sighed heavily. "Jasper brought up an excellent point last night. The Germans started all of this by clearing out every resistance cell in the vicinity. How did they know where to find you? Were they aware of your presence beforehand, or did someone give them a handful of addresses all at once? In the end, the details don't matter. The vital thing is that someone must have shared the information. For so many operations to be compromised and attacked on the same night, it suggests a mole."

"And you suspect Minuit?"

"I do not know. But I find it unusual that we find the one cell in all of France that has a wolf in it."

Sandrine said, "Minuit didn't know she was a wolf until we told her. You were the one who sent us to Meldeuses. So if her existence is too coincidental, the only one I'm suspicious of is you."

Simon held up his hand. "Stop. Stop it this instant. I will not have us fighting one another at a time like this. Sandrine, do you trust Min?"

"I do. With my life."

"And I trust Kenneth. If there is a traitor providing information to the enemy, they are not in this car."

Sandrine said, "And if the traitor is back at Meldeuses, we just sent Irene and Leopold back to alert them of our plan. If there are Nazis in the factory, they'll be watching for us."

"I am well aware of that possibility," Simon said. "But there's nothing we can do about that. We must investigate this lead, and we require the help of our friends and allies. We cannot leave them on the sidelines just because one might be a collaborator."

"You may be gambling with our lives," Min said.

"Welcome to the war."

Sandrine snorted and looked out the window. It was forty-one kilometers to Saint-Pierre-Aigle. Everything in him said that an entire division of Germans would be waiting for them when they arrived. It didn't matter if the enemy got an early warning about their arrival. No matter what happened, he doubted their pack would survive the coming attack. He couldn't plan in a way that everyone walked out unscathed, so he had to prepare for casualties.

This was the reason he and the rest of the pack survived that night in Monthyon. He'd been kept alive so he could complete the ultimate mission and save countless lives by preventing the birth of a new hell on earth. For that, his life was a small price to pay.

CHAPTER FIFTEEN

THEY FOUND an abandoned barn not far from Saint-Pierre-Aigle where they could stash the car. Simon parked between the long-empty stalls and covered it with a tarp while the others stripped down. Min was apprehensive about undressing in front of two strange men, so Sandrine casually stepped in front of her to block their line of sight. She didn't bother telling the girl she had nothing to worry about; Simon and Kenneth were both homosexual, and true *canidae* tended to not give a damn about communal nudity. They both transformed into their wolves, leaving the women on two legs.

"Are you ready?"

"I am. I've just never forced myself to do it before. Not when it really mattered."

Sandrine looked at the men. They turned and scurried from the barn to leave the women alone. Sandrine put her hands on Min's shoulders and leaned in to whisper into her ear.

"You are a beautiful girl, but I want to see your wolf. I want to see you let go, embrace your primal side. You've been holding back for too long. It wants to be free. It wants to run wild and experience life. Stop holding it back. Stop caging your true nature. You can feel it can't you? Bursting at the seams? Normally you can hold it back, but ever since you gave in, you've wanted more. So take it, Minuit. Take everything you've ever deprived yourself of and surrender. Let it out. I want to see it." She nipped Min's earlobe. "Show me your wolf."

Min groaned and pulled back just enough to find Sandrine's lips with her own. Sandrine closed her eyes and cupped Min's face with her hands, forcing her back until she was pinned to the wall. Their skin rippled as they kissed, and Min rolled her head back to moan painfully. "It hurts!"

"Stop fighting it. Relax." She kissed Min's face, brushing her lips over the smooth skin of her cheek until it began to thicken. Hair sprouted from her pelt, and Min shoved her away. Sandrine stumbled and fell to her knees, hands splayed on the ground seconds before they turned into paws. She arched her back and stretched her neck out, letting her spine twisted and rearrange her form. Min dropped down next to her and shook her fur, turning to look at her tail before she pressed her snout against Sandrine's neck.

Sandrine nudged Min's head away, then turned and bounded outside. Min followed her. Simon and Kenneth had ventured several yards away from the barn and began running when they saw their companions were ready. Sandrine broke into a run as well, looking back only once to make sure Min was keeping up. The girl had a long and elegant stride, head down and tail up as she pushed through the tall grass. Obviously the wolf was indeed overjoyed to finally have a chance to run free. Sandrine cut to one side and slammed against Min, almost knocking her off her feet. Min stumbled and tripped over her own feet, yelped in surprise and shock, then snapped her jaws at Sandrine's tail. Sandrine dodged out of the way just in time and pranced forward, loping across the uneven ground.

Simon stopped at the tree line and yapped twice. Sandrine acknowledged his scolding and stopped fooling around. Min's enthusiasm was understandable. She was young, free for the first time, and with a whole new pack. But Sandrine had no excuse for her exuberance. They had a mission ahead of them. She needed to be focused and keep her head in the game. It was no time to be playing around.

The four of them entered the woods with Min leading the way.

She was the only one who'd seen the porcelain factory before, so they were relying on her to save them from wandering blindly. Sandrine brought up the rear so she could keep watch for any incoming vehicles, German or otherwise. The road was a pitted and worn-down gray ribbon laid down through the woods. Up ahead, the trees disappeared behind a thick veil of fog that left the asphalt under their paws slick with moisture. They ran south until the woods on either side of them had grown so thick it was impossible to see beyond them. All around was green and brown, with only a narrow strip of gray sky visible directly above them.

Soon, the ground also began to rise. Muddy cliffs sloped up on either side of the road until it felt as if they were actually going underground. Their breath clouded around their faces as they ran. Four wolves panting, their paws tapping a frantic drum beat. Up ahead the road branched off, and Min paused for only the briefest of moments before choosing the left path.

After making her choice they only ran for ten more minutes before she came to a stop and moved to the side of the road. Sandrine didn't have to ask; she could smell that they had arrived at their destination. Vehicle exhaust, the smell of sawdust and construction, and the smell of food being cooked meant a large group was camped out nearby. Simon guided them off the road and into the woods, traveling along a layer of leaves that had been crushed to mulch in the muddy ground.

When he stopped, he immediately began to transform. He leaned against a tree, crouching as a naked and sweaty human being, and pointed up ahead as the others changed as well.

"Looks like the whelp was right."

Sandrine looked out and had to swallow the bile rising in her throat. The porcelain factory was a massive structure, a squat two-story building that looked like an eagle perched on the grass with both wings outspread. Most of the Palladian windows were smashed free of glass, but someone was in the process of repairing them all. From their vantage point she could see four buildings behind the main structure, all in various states of disrepair and decrepitude. But a squadron of Germans were buzzing around the shattered remnants of the building like bees. They carried tools and supplies, some of them stripped down to their underclothes despite the chill temperature.

"I assume it didn't look like this when you last saw it," Kenneth said.

Min didn't respond. Sandrine looked at her and followed the girl's stare. Simon and Kenneth were both crouching, their semi-erect cocks hanging between their thighs in full view. Sandrine knew the odds were good that it was the first time Min had ever seen a man naked, let alone two at the same time. She reached out and snapped her fingers next to Min's ear.

"Focus."

"Right. Sorry. No. No, they're... all the repairs. They're new."

Kenneth looked at Simon. "Do you have any ideas?"

"I'm going down there to get a closer look. The rest of you fall back to the barn. If you don't hear from me by nightfall, assume the worst."

"Nightfall?" Sandrine said. "That's hours from now."

He shrugged. "I want to be sure I get a good look. Assume I've been captured and wait for the others to arrive. Surround this place and do everything you can to burn it to the ground."

Kenneth said, "With you still inside?"

Simon said, "Destroying this place now at the cost of my own life, weighed against the number of lives that will be lost here if we let it stand. I don't see any other choice."

Kenneth grunted. "Just the same, do your best to get out in one piece."

"Always." He dropped his hands to the ground and transformed again. He stretched out his hind legs and moved cautiously toward the slope with his belly scraping through the mud.

Sandrine didn't know if she or Kenneth were in charge now that Simon was gone. Rather than asking, she said, "All right. Let's get somewhere safer." She stood and walked deeper into the woods. A few seconds later she heard Kenneth and Min get up to follow her.

Simon skidded down the incline using his forelegs as rudders to steer around obstacles. When he reached the bottom he looked back to see Kenneth watching him. The Brit gave a thumbs-up and then disappeared from view. Simon scanned the area to make sure he hadn't been spotted and darted across the field. The factory was surrounded by a tall drab wall of gray stone. He lurked along the perimeter until he found a gate with iron staves set far enough apart for him to slip through. It was a tight fit but he quickly made it through and dropped out into a stretch of cracked pavement. He was between two buildings with clay tile roofs. A wheelbarrow overflowing with construction debris stood nearby.

He moved forward while scenting the air for guards or workmen. The area he was currently in reeked of cigarette smoke and the barest traces of food, leading him to believe it was a break area. Up ahead was an intersection that ran along the back of another building. He was surrounded by the tightly-packed buildings and the paths between them formed a maddening maze of dead-ends and turnarounds. He tried to stay close to the wall so he wouldn't lose his bearings, but it was difficult with all the people he was forced to dodge.

After ten minutes he felt like he had a pretty good idea of the layout. There was the large building that fronted the road, then a cluster of eight or nine smaller buildings corralled behind it by the stone wall. It was a modern fortress, protected but nowhere near impregnable. With a force of the right size, they could swarm it from all directions. Wolves and humans working in congress could do a lot of damage. Once the soldiers currently working on-site were dealt with, they would have plenty of time to demolish the building before Hitler could send any reinforcements.

"*Alter Schwede!*"

Simon turned toward the voice, ready to make an escape, but every available route was cut off. The German soldier's gun was resting casually against his chest. Simon knew he could have it up and ready to fire in a second. Another soldier appeared in response to the first's shout. Simon backed up and kept his eyes on the approaching soldiers. They chattered to each other without taking their eyes off their quarry. The first one smiled reassuringly and held up his hand.

There were a handful of options. He could attack the closest soldier, but the second would shoot him before he could get away. He could just make a run for it and hope they didn't pursue. Or he could play docile and hope for a better chance to escape. The first soldier knelt down and nervously reached out to put his hand on top of Simon's head. He petted it roughly and then laughed.

"*Schauen, er ist sanft,*" he said. "*Dies ist ein gutes omen. Ulrich wird wissen wollen.*"

Simon only knew a bit of German, but he picked out Ulrich's name immediately. He popped up on his hind legs, startling the soldier into pulling his hand back. The man laughed off his fright and stood to take a step back.

"*Ich glaube er den Kommandanten treffen will. Lass uns gehen, pup.*"

"*Das ist ein wildes tier!*"

The first soldier scoffed and shook his head. "*Komm schon, wolfie.*" He clicked his tongue and patted his thigh. Simon relaxed his posture and moved closer. He laughed and gestured at Simon.

"*Ein gutter Hund.*"

Simon followed the two soldiers out of the dead-end he'd trapped himself in. Now that he couldn't evade and hide, the factory seemed to be swarming with the enemy. They all paused to look at the animal in their midst, gawking until he and his captors were out of sight. He wondered if the soldier would just stand aside and let him go or if he was supposed to become the camp's mascot. Either way, he knew Kenneth would follow the plan.

They went into the main building that was reminiscent of a castle. Sounds of construction echoed down the stone corridors, and he could hear German men shouting orders to one another. One man was singing over the sound of hammering. Simon fought the urge to sneeze at the clouds of sawdust that filled the air, and the soldier clicked his tongue again to guide Simon into a side room.

As soon as they crossed the threshold, Simon felt as if he was in a completely different building. The floor was covered with thick carpeting. There was furniture, pristine as if it had been covered by a drop cloth just before they arrived. Directly ahead of them was a massive oak desk that looked like the prow of a ship, and behind it was a framed landscape. Somewhere in Germany, if Simon had to guess. A Victrola was playing in the corner; the music was incongruously soothing and gentle.

Seated behind the desk was *Oberst* Karl Ulrich. It was the demon responsible for killing Philip, the man who would be in charge of a concentration camp that would cause the death of thousands.

He looked weak. He looked pathetic. The collar of his uniform was too wide for his neck, leaving a gap between skin and cloth that made him appear childish. His jaw was well-formed and his forehead bulbous, the dark blonde hair receding almost to the middle of his head. He wore thin-framed glasses and pursed his lips prissily when he realized he was being interrupted. He looked up, eyes wide and blue like a baby's, and he furrowed his brow when he saw the wolf.

Simon used his scant knowledge of German to assume what the men were saying. "What in the hell is this?" Ulrich asked, gesturing at Simon with three fingers.

"I found it on the grounds, *Oberst*. He is very docile." He patted Simon's head again. "I thought it was a sign. Wolves... wolves are fierce creatures. And to find one here is... is..."

"You believe the fates gave us this wolf as a symbol that they support our cause?"

"That is exactly it. Yes sir."

Ulrich shook his head and went back to writing. His hands were slender and frail, an artist's hands. "Get that beast out of here before it soils my carpet."

"Of course. My apologies."

Ulrich ignored the soldier and focused on what he was doing. The soldier moved toward the door. "Come on. Come. Wolfie, come."

Simon walked up to Ulrich's desk and stared at him. The German finally realized he was being observed and looked into the wolf's eyes. Something he saw there gave him pause, and he tilted his head to one side. Simon didn't blink, didn't shrink away. Even in his wolf form, he could tell the message was getting through to the German prick behind the desk.

"It is a *faszinierende kreatur*," Ulrich muttered.

Simon envisioned ripping out the man's delicate throat, feeling its warm blood spray over his face and skin. The soldier wrapped an arm around Simon's neck and pulled him away from the desk. He chanted weak, ineffectual apologies to Ulrich as he dragged the wild animal out of his superior's office. Simon managed to look back to see the *oberst* still watching him.

His vision of killing the Nazi wasn't just wishful thinking. It was a prophecy, one that he intended to bring to reality as soon as possible.

CHAPTER SIXTEEN

SIMON THOUGHT the soldier might try to keep him as a pet - he heard the word "*gelehrig*" and "domesticated" - but he was led to the main gates so he could be released. Their path took them through parts of the compound he hadn't seen while sneaking around and he tried to see as much as possible without being obvious about it. He hadn't kept anywhere near an accurate count, but he could presume there were at least fifty armed men on the grounds. They all looked bored, but he couldn't decide if that was a pro or a con. Bored soldiers could fall asleep, or they could be eager for something to get their attention. Simon was fortunate his new friend hadn't seen a sneaky wolf as an opportunity for target practice.

The screeching of the gate hurt Simon's ears as it was pushed open. He was led down the road to where the trees began. The soldier crouched in front of him and patted him on the side of the head.

"Looks like *Oberst* Ulrich isn't superstitious. Too bad. We could have used a mascot. But the others will be glad to know about your little visit." He grinned, showing his teeth. "Wolves are powerful and free. Thank you for coming to visit us, pup. You've given us all hope that God is on our side."

Simon lunged forward. He turned his head sideways and sunk his teeth into the German's face. He twisted his whole body and felt muscle and flesh tearing, his mouth flooding with blood as the young man collapsed in the grass. Simon spit the nauseating mouthful out and looked at the boy's mauled head, trying not to focus too much on the specific damage he had just caused. The soldier's ripped upper lip flooded with bubbling blood, indicating he was still trying to draw breath. Simon stepped onto the man's chest and tore out his throat. The soldier died with a weak gurgle.

He didn't want to risk transforming to go through the soldier's pockets, even though he knew there might be something worth having in them. If the body was ransacked, the other soldiers might suspect foul play. As it was, they'd all seen him parading through the facility with a wild animal. Ulrich and everyone else would just assume he'd been foolish enough to play with a wolf he'd found in the forest and had paid the ultimate price.

With a quick look around, Simon slipped into the forest and used the trees to cover his escape. He remembered seeing a river on the map. He let the wolf's senses guide him to the water and ran off the muddy banks. He dunked his head under and let the current wash the blood from his muzzle before he transformed. Blood and gristle wasn't too bad as the wolf, but if it was still there when he changed, it would nauseate him.

Once he was sufficiently clean, he ran through the river to the other side. He knew where he was, and he had a general idea where to find the barn where the others were waiting.

Min wanted to wait as long as possible to return to her "normal" shape. She was reluctant to feel the ache in her joints that she was starting to associate with the shift, but that wasn't the only reason. Her mind reeled with what she had just done. It was her first true exploration of being a wolf and she was sad that it was nearly over. Before she would hide in her room, fighting every instinct that begged to go out into the night. She just wanted to ride out the monster tearing itself out of her body once a month. She wanted to hide her shame.

Now that she knew the truth she wanted to beg the wolf to forgive her. If only she had known what it was like to run free and wild under a canopy of trees. The smells of the forest and the scurrying of tiny animals nearby that saw her as a predator to be feared. She couldn't imagine tearing apart a bunny or vole, but sensing them nearby was a shockingly great experience.

Perhaps part of her enjoyment came from the company she shared. Stoic Simon and silent Sandrine had transformed in more ways than the physical. They were quick and dynamic, bursting with energy. Even Kenneth had a different spirit about him when he was running on four legs.

But they had arrived at the barn, and she knew she had no excuse to remain as the wolf. She watched as Kenneth pushed the door shut behind them. He looked skinny in clothes, but naked she could see the play of muscles under his skin as he walked the sliding door into place. His arms and shoulders flexed beautifully, and his thighs bulged with each step. And her eyes dropped to his cock, semi-erect between his legs. She'd never seen one before, and now she had seen two in the space of an hour. She was certainly curious about it, but her true focus was on Sandrine.

She turned to see the gorgeous wolf-woman walking toward her. She had put on a shirt that hung low enough to cover the dark hair between her legs, but Min could still picture every curve of the older woman's body. The dark nipples, the flat stomach with a scar on the lower right side. The blemishes were beautiful. The long stretches of naked skin made her crave a taste. Now that she knew how to fully appreciate her stronger senses, she wanted to put them to proper use.

Kenneth turned and walked toward her, nonchalant about being exposed in front of her. His skin was sweaty and the skin still seemed to ripple from his change. She knew then that she truly wasn't attracted to men, because all she felt looking at him was a sense of a wasted opportunity.

"Are you going to join us, or do you want to be the wolf all day?"

She wasn't quite as casual with her nudity as her companions, but she transformed anyway. She stretched her arms out to either side and balanced on the balls of her feet. Her body felt like putting on an old pair of shoes, letting herself fill the old familiar corners before it settled into itself. She looked down and ran her hand over the curve of her hips, moving one hand to cover her crotch as she crossed the other arm over her breasts. Sandrine handed her a coat, and Min gratefully pulled it on.

"So what do we do? Just... wait?"

"There's not much else we can do," Kenneth said. He had retrieved his clothes from the car and stepped into his pants. "Now that we know for sure what we're dealing with, we can start to plan. Simon will provide us with more detail when he gets back, but we've confirmed the Nazis are holed up in the factory. We need to start thinking of how we're going to stop them from using it."

"A fire." It was the first thing Sandrine had said since regaining her human form, and the sound of her voice startled Min.

Kenneth said, "Those buildings are brick and stone. Did you see the shingles on the outer buildings? Those prevent fire from spreading. That whole place was built to withstand fire. That's probably one of the selling points for the damn Jerries. If you're going to burn someone alive, you want your fortress to hold up under high temperatures."

Min leaned against the side of the car. She knew she should put on some more clothes, or at least button up the jacket. But she enjoyed being casually naked. She wanted to be as comfortable with it as Kenneth and Sandrine apparently were. She had never been naked with anyone before. Sandrine was still not wearing pants. Kenneth was shirtless. Min watched them as they talked and imagined Sandrine's lips on Kenneth's chest. Her tongue running over his nipples. Dropping onto her knees and licking his stomach. She chewed her lip and squeezed her thighs together as she envisioned it.

"We'll have a better idea of what we can do when the rest of our group arrives. The plan might be simple. When we have gathered in force, we'll gauge whether we can swarm the camp from all sides. We'll kill the Germans on-site and take our time making this place useless to anyone else who comes along. Simon will also be able to tell us how many enemy soldiers we have to face."

Min said, "What if... what if we're..." She swallowed and looked down at her bare feet, caked with mud from their long run. She wondered how it remained on her skin when the pelt retracted to... wherever it went. She curled her toes under and looked at them again. "What if I can't murder?"

Sandrine said, "We won't ask you to do that if you're not comfortable with it. There will certainly be other jobs you can have."

Kenneth nodded. "Of course. No one will force you to kill if you aren't ready for it."

"Thank you. I will make myself useful in other ways. I swear it."

"Minuit, you have nothing to prove. You are the entire reason we know this place exists. Did you see that valley it was in? These woods all around us? It would have been the easiest thing in the world to overlook that factory. We may have found it eventually, but never in time to make a difference. You found it for us. You put us in the right place. Your work can be done now if you like. You could go home tonight and know you have played a vital role in winning this war."

Min blinked in surprise and chuckled shyly. "I think that's the most I've heard you speak."

Sandrine took a slow breath. "Perhaps. I am not averse to speaking. I simply believe it should only be done when necessary. Words have value, and I'm not comfortable spending more than my share."

Kenneth said, "Their value is immaterial when you spend them so well."

Sandrine grimaced and turned away.

Kenneth smiled. "We can discuss this over food. I'm sure Min here is famished after her first real run."

Min returned his smile. "Yes, very much so."

He retrieved the rations from the car. There was extremely little food to go around; a bite or two of meat, even less cheese, and a relatively large hunk of bread. Min took her share and went to sit against the wall. She spread the material of her coat over her lap and began tearing pieces off the food. With the right amount of portioning she could make five tiny sandwiches. If she chewed those carefully enough she could fool herself into thinking she had eaten more than she really had. They had plenty of Jerusalem artichokes, and if she was still hungry she would mash up one for a midnight snack, but she would wait until her hunger became dire.

Sandrine came to sit next to her while Kenneth went into the loft. There was an opening there he could open just enough to see if anyone was coming. Sandrine watched Min prepare her food and then popped her portion of meat into her mouth all at once. She chewed slowly, though, staring at nothing across from them. Min tried to follow her lead. There was hay all over the ground, leftover from when it was a working barn, and she could smell animals and their shit. She wondered if that was part of the wolf coming out, then chided herself. Of course it was.

"Sandrine? What happened last night? That was... um..." She chewed her bottom lip. "I liked that a lot. It was the first time anything like that had happened." She felt herself blushing and fought the urge to cover her face. "I enjoyed it very much."

Sandrine nodded.

"I want it to happen again."

Sandrine looked at her.

"As soon as we can. I know that tomorrow or whenever the others get here, we're going to attack that camp. And I know that a lot of us will probably die. Even if I'm not in the fighting, I could die. And you could definitely die, because I know you'll be out there in the thick of it. And I don't know if I'd want to do it as much if it wasn't with you. I want you to fuck me tonight, Sandrine, just in case we don't get another opportunity."

She was breathing hard, nervous to have spouted so much secret stuff all at once. Her hands were shaking and she was afraid she might dump her food onto the ground if she moved.

"I'd like that too, Minuit."

Min smiled broadly. "Okay." She looked up into the loft. "What if... Simon and Kenneth will be here, too. What if they are here when... when we're..."

"Then they'll hear. Do you have a problem with that?"

"No."

"Good. Eat your meal."

Min picked up one of her tiny sandwiches and put it on her tongue. In the past few years she'd gotten good at making the smallest portions last. She held it in her mouth and rolled it across her teeth. She sometimes wondered how she would fare if she was given a full portion, a meal fit for a queen, and she realized she would probably only eat a tenth of it. She had forgotten what it was like to be full. The sensation was worse now, when her mind was on anything but eating.

She was extraordinarily excited and anxious for what the night held. She knew the next day would be impossibly dangerous. It might be her last day breathing. But she knew it wouldn't matter if she spent the night properly and with the right person. She reached over and brushed her finger over the back of Sandrine's hand. Sandrine pulled her hand away at the first touch.

"This isn't going to be romantic."

"Yes, it is." Sandrine looked at her. "It is, Sandrine. It's not just because I want to die knowing what it's like to have sex. For that I could have anybody. I want it to be with you. It has to be with you. That makes it romantic. Right?"

Sandrine faced forward and said nothing. Min also looked forward.

Just as she was about to give up hope, Sandrine moved her hand to link her fingers with Min's.

CHAPTER SEVENTEEN

KENNETH ANNOUNCED Simon's return as soon as he saw the wolf break through the underbrush. It was dusk, and the sun was casting long shadows across the fields. All three of them had been anxious due to Simon's deadline of "nightfall," but none of them admitted it by expressing relief at his return.

By the time Simon reached the barn, Kenneth had climbed down the ladder and pushed the door open. Simon entered at a run and skidded to a stop, shuddering as he shrunk in around himself and rose in human form. He shook his arms and flexed his fingers, brushing the detritus of the barn floor from his palms. Min had taken Simon's clothes from the car and stepped forward to hand them over. He took them, noticed that she was staring openly at his naked body, and then turned away. Sandrine smirked; the girl was getting bolder in her appreciations.

"How did things go?"

"Better and worse than we could have hoped," Simon said as he dressed. "I was captured while exploring their camp, but I was taken to see Ulrich himself. Now we know that he is actually on-site, and I know where his office is within the compound."

Kenneth said, "You were captured? How did you manage to get away?"

"The foolish boy who captured me thought I was an omen. He wanted me to be their totem, but Ulrich ordered him to release me. I didn't want the idiot telling everyone the gods had blessed their godforsaken plan, so when he led me back to the forest, I killed him." Kenneth started to protest. "It would look like a wolf attack. A half-dozen people saw him parading around a wild animal. They'll think he deserved it."

Sandrine said, "And it's one less soldier we'll have to fight when we attack."

Simon nodded. "What happened here? Have we heard anything from Leopold or the others?"

"Not yet," Kenneth said.

"Fine. We'll bed down here for the night. Sandrine, you and Min get some rest. I'll take first watch. Kenneth will relieve me, then Sandrine and Min. Does that work for everyone?"

They agreed to the schedule, and Simon took his portion of dinner up to the loft. Kenneth looked at Sandrine and Min. "I'll do a perimeter walk, make sure nothing is sneaking up on us from the south. You ladies can take the car if you wish."

"Thank you, Kenneth," Min said, looking down at her feet rather than either of the others.

Kenneth smiled at Sandrine, who nodded her thanks to him. She followed him to the door so she could latch it behind him. Min wet her lips and swallowed nervously as Sandrine walked back to her. She was so elegant, strong, and frightening in a very appealing way. "Are you ready for bed?"

"Yes." She rubbed her hands on the hem of her jacket and let Sandrine lead her to the car. The back door had been standing open since they were using it as their pantry. Sandrine moved everything to the front passenger seat before she slid inside. Min joined her and shut the door as quietly as she could. The entire barn was dark, but Sandrine stretched between the front seats and turned on the flashlight. It flickered and died until she smacked it against her palm a few times. Once it was glowing steadily, she set it so the beam shone against the floor. The backwash of light was enough to see by without making them feel like they were in a spotlight.

"Won't that kill the battery?"

Sandrine said, "Probably. But it's dying anyway, so we probably wouldn't use it for anything mission-related. And if we're in wolf form, we can see better in the dark than humans can. The group from Meldeuses will be bringing more torches when they come."

"Oh."

"And that is all justification for the fact that I want to see you when I'm fucking you."

Min's ears burned. "O-oh." She was very aware of the men lingering in the area. She doubted Kenneth would be able to hear anything from outside, but he knew exactly what they were doing. Soon Simon would know as well. She expected to be anxious about their presence, but she was more surprised that she didn't care. She wanted them to listen. She wanted them to know what she was going to do, and letting them hear it saved her the trouble of bragging.

They sat side by side without speaking until Sandrine reached over and touched Min's knee. She moved her hand slowly up the inside of Min's leg, each centimeter an opportunity for Min to say no or to stop what was happening. Min curled her fingers on the cuffs of her jacket sleeves, struggling to keep her breathing steady as her heart threatened to go into overdrive. She thought maybe it had been knocked out of rhythm, taking two beats at once and then waiting too long to take another, and it made her shake. Sandrine drew a circle on the very top of Min's thigh, then moved her hand away from Min's sex.

"Wait..."

"Sh." Sandrine pulled Min to her, turning so that her weight was resting against Sandrine's thigh. Sandrine put her arm around Min's waist. Min put one foot on the seat, left the other in the floor, and settled against Sandrine's body. She could feel Sandrine's breasts against her back, the warmth of her breath on her neck, and most of all the weight of the older woman's hand moving back to her thigh. She trembled and looked down. Sandrine dragged the backs of her fingers through Min's pubic hair. She brought her hand up and touched Min's mouth. Min kissed the pad of Sandrine's index finger.

"No. Suck them. Make them wet."

Min took two fingers into her mouth and swirled her tongue around them. As she did, Sandrine bowed her head and kissed

Min's neck.

"I am humbled to be your first partner, Minuit," Sandrine whispered, "and I will be honored if you are my last."

"Sandrine..."

"Sh." She moved her hand back down. Min covered it with her own and gasped when Sandrine's fingers found her sex. She parted the hair covering it and gently pushed her finger inside. It was different than it had been the night before. Not because she was mostly naked, and not just because of what they'd said to each other, but because it truly felt like sex. Their first encounter had been a precursor to this, just foreplay, but now she knew she was finally going to cross that threshold. Sandrine pulled her finger out and brushed it over the sensitive flesh.

"Do you feel this?"

"Uhm-hmm..."

"That's where I want you to put your tongue on me. Do you think you can do that, Minuit?"

She swallowed the lump in her throat. "Yes." She started to move, but Sandrine used her free hand to push her back down.

"No. You're first." Her fingers curled around the material of the coat and pulled it aside. She dropped her hand to Min's exposed breast and circled the nipple as she gently worked her finger in and out, pausing with just the tip inside so she could add a second finger. Min hissed through her teeth but whispered she was okay before Sandrine could ask. Her real fear was hyperventilating or passing out. Sandrine was kissing her neck, fondling her breast, fucking her, and any one of those things would have been enough to make her weak. All three at once, and she didn't know how she was still forming rational thoughts.

Min wrapped her arm around Sandrine's leg and fell backward, draping herself across Sandrine's lap. Sandrine let her fall and continued rubbing with her palm, thrusting with her fingers. Min looked up at the gorgeous and mysterious woman who had appeared in her life like a cannon blast. Dark and frightening in all the best ways, holding open the doors Min had been trying to hold shut for years. For the first time Min felt not only like an adult, but like a person. The person she was meant to be.

"*Je t'aime*," Min whispered, the last syllable sullied by a moan.

She arched her back and Sandrine dragged her free hand over Min's breasts, baring them both before resting her hand on the hard bone between them. Min's body was bowed, her head against the seat on one side of Sandrine's lap as her hips lifted off the opposite side. She pressed down on the hand still working between her legs, toes curling. She clapped a hand over her own mouth to stifle the sounds coming out of her, choked gasps that sounded like surprise and shock all at once.

When she dropped her hand away, Sandrine bent down and kissed her. Min melted, the tension in her body dissipating out her toes and fingers and through her mouth as she succumbed to the kiss. She felt Sandrine's tongue in her mouth and welcomed it, reaching up to put her hands in the thick dark hair hanging over Sandrine's shoulder.

"*Je t'aime*, Minuit."

Sandrine's voice was softer than Min had ever heard it, and she could tell she had just gotten a glimpse of who Sandrine was pre-war. She moved her hand to Sandrine's cheek, stretching out her thumb to brush it over Sandrine's lips. Sandrine kissed it and then turned her head to press her mouth against Min's palm. She kissed down to her wrist and scraped her teeth over the tender skin there. She eased the spot she'd bitten with her tongue, and then looked up.

"Can I do... th-the thing now?"

Sandrine chuckled. It was practically full-throated laughter, something that Min would have thought foreign to Sandrine before that moment.

"Yes, Minuit."

They rearranged themselves in the backseat. Sandrine twisted to rest her back against the door, and Min rolled onto her stomach. Sandrine had one leg against the seat, the other on the floor, and Min settled easily between her thighs. She breathed deeply before pressing her face against the dark hair over Sandrine's mound. She could become addicted to that smell if she wasn't careful. She pressed kisses to the hair, tasting the wetness and knowing it was because of her. Sandrine put a hand on the side of her head and politely guided her lower.

Min opened her mouth wide and dragged her tongue over the

puffy flesh, her chin trembling. The smell was almost too much for her to take, but she forced herself to focus. She looked up and saw Sandrine looking at her. Sandrine nodded encouragingly and whispered to her what to do. Sandrine used her lips and tongue to find the clitoris, then brought up her fingers and wetted them as well. She was shaking all over now; worried about doing it wrong, worried about making a mistake because she wasn't paying close enough attention, worried it wouldn't be perfect.

One look at Sandrine, however, proved she didn't have anything to fear. Perfect or not, she was on the verge of orgasm. Min pressed the flat of her tongue against Sandrine's clit and brought her hand up to her chin. She extended her thumb and pressed it between Sandrine's lips, rubbing as she licked and kissed, and suddenly Sandrine bucked against her.

"Minuit... yes..."

Min smiled and continued her assault until Sandrine pushed her away. Min stretched up along Sandrine's body and settled on top of her. They found each other's lips and kissed eagerly. Sandrine moaned when Min settled her hip against Sandrine's sex.

"Sorry..."

"No, don't. Don't you dare move."

Min kissed Sandrine's chin. "Now what?"

"Now we can do it again. Or we can sleep." She kissed Min's cheeks and chin. "I vote for sleep."

"Me too."

Sandrine stroked Min's hair, guided her head to her chest, and sighed. Min smiled and told herself that she was going to stay awake as long as possible, but she was asleep before the flashlight died.

CHAPTER EIGHTEEN

WHEN SIMON climbed down the ladder to let Kenneth back inside, the car was gently rocking back and forth with a gentle, rhythmic creak. He couldn't remember the last time Sandrine had been fucked, and he could tell she had feelings for the little blonde one. He could think of no better time to consummate their flirtation than before going into battle. It would clear their minds and focus their energies for the attack on Ulrich's camp, and he only hoped they left themselves enough time to sleep before dawn.

Kenneth slipped into the barn. "We're all..." He looked toward the car. They had turned on a flashlight, and its dim glow was enough to see several quite intriguing silhouettes against the dirty glass of the back window. "Clear. Well. They didn't waste any time, did they?"

"Time isn't something we have in abundance."

"No. More power to them. Not to speak out of turn, but Sandrine needs someone like that girl in her life. Energetic and enthusiastic. And I believe Minuit needs someone like Sandrine. They complement each other well."

They had been speaking in whispers as they moved past the car, but neither thought the occupants would have noticed even if they spoke in full voice. Simon climbed up the ladder to his perch and, so he wouldn't feel as if he was intruding on Sandrine and Min's privacy any more than necessary, Kenneth followed him up. The loft door was open enough so Simon could see out, and the gap was currently allowing in a sliver of icy gray moonlight. Simon walked over to sit against the wall. Kenneth walked to the edge of the loft and tested the banister to see if it would bear his weight. He decided it was safe and rested his hands on it.

Below, the car had stopped moving. Silence filled the barn. Simon's head was turned so he could see outside, one hand resting on his holstered gun.

"They have the right idea, you know."

"Hm."

"You don't agree?"

Simon said, "I didn't say that. Philip and I used to prepare missions in bed. We would celebrate a mission gone well in the same way."

The creaking began again.

Kenneth looked down at the car in disbelief. "Bloody hell. I suppose they both do have a wolf's stamina, but that's rather impressive."

"It's been ages since Sandrine had a lover. I'm not surprised she's a bit... insatiable." He reached down to adjust his pants. The noises from below, as well as their topic of conversation, had made him think of Philip. Their nights together after Irene helped him realize where his true passions lie. They were always electric in bed, but there had been a superstitious quality to their lovemaking the nights before a big mission. Being inside someone he loved, the feel of someone else's orgasm at his hand, made him feel spiritual. Made him feel imbued with something beyond human, beyond the wolf.

He lifted his hand from the weapon and flexed his fingers. He told himself it was just the cold, but he felt unsettled. Itchy and uncomfortable. He knew how he would burn off the tension if he was alone, or if Philip had still been there... He squeezed his eyes shut and aborted that thought before it could fully form. It had been six months. Half a year since Philip was taken from him. He should think about the present. He should be focusing on what he'd seen of the camp, planning, scheming.

Sandrine cried out from the lower level and Kenneth exhaled

sharply. "They're quite, ah..." He cleared his throat.

"No one can hear them outside of this barn. Unless they are also wolves, in which case they'd smell us long before they heard anything. Let them have their fun."

"No one is saying they shouldn't be doing it," Kenneth said. "Just that it's... distracting."

Simon looked over as the British officer adjusted his pants as well. It did little to hide the bulge rising beneath his zipper, and Simon suddenly decided Sandrine had the right thought in more ways than one. He didn't want to admit his attraction to the Brit for several reasons. Having the officer forced into his pack being the main issue, but he'd be lying if he said it was the only one. Six months on his own, and in walked this beautiful, dashing British wolf? For the first time he allowed himself to consider what Philip would have done if he was still alive when Officer Kenneth Mackay dropped into their lives.

Philip would have looked the man up and down and, the first opportunity he had to speak privately with his lover, he would have said, "We're going to ravish that teabag as soon as possible."

He chuckled quietly to himself.

"What's so funny?"

He started to dismiss the question, but he looked outside. On the other side of those trees was a death camp waiting to start slaughtering people. At the moment, he and the trio of soldiers in the barn with him were the only thing preventing it from that purpose. Philip would throw him out the loft window if he knew Simon was denying himself relief out of misplaced loyalty for a dead partner. Philip would tell him to take care of himself first.

"Come over here, Mackay."

Kenneth approached cautiously. "I thought we were all Loupin."

"Well, right now you're Mackay."

Simon got onto his knees and reached for Kenneth's belt. Kenneth's hands twitched as if he intended to stop what was happening, but he gave up before he even tried. The belt buckle jingled quietly as it was released, and Simon unfastened the buttons of his pants. He put his hand inside and squeezed the front of Kenneth's underwear. He felt the shaft swell against his fingers, warm and thick. His hands shook as he pushed the cotton out of his way and freed the erection. It fell against his mouth and he pressed a kiss to the side of it, using the tip of his tongue to trace back up to the head.

Kenneth grunted and put his hand on Simon's shoulder. He lifted his eyes and looked straight ahead through the gap in the loft door. The moon was nearly full and he felt like he could see as far as if the sun was out. The woods were unnaturally still. He could hear the car moving down below and, if he focused, he could also hear sounds coming from within. Whimpers and moans. He moved his hand from Simon's shoulder to the back of his head, running his fingers through the thick hair before grabbing a handful of it.

Simon closed his lips over the tip of Kenneth's cock, holding it just long enough to wet it with his tongue before letting it fall free. He looped two fingers around the base and stroked it, letting it brush over his mouth without actually taking it inside. He wanted to spend the entire night exploring its length, reminding himself what it was like to have a cock in his mouth, but he knew it wouldn't be fair to Kenneth to draw it out that long.

He used his tongue to guide it to his lips, and he pressed a soft kiss to the tip of it. His tongue curled around it as Kenneth gently thrust forward. Simon tugged down Kenneth's pants, and his underwear quickly followed. He stopped just long enough to wet two fingers and put his hand between Kenneth's legs. Kenneth grunted as Simon pressed his middle finger against his ass while sucking on the head of his cock, alternating between suction and pressure.

Kenneth was breathing heavily, almost hyperventilating. He moved his hands to the placket of his shirt, giving his fumbling fingers the job of undoing the buttons. When they were all open, he dropped the material and returned his hands to Simon's beautiful, thick hair. Simon took him deep, relaxing his throat so he could take the full length into his mouth at once before pulling back.

Kenneth felt his orgasm approaching but he didn't want to end the moment so soon. When Simon tried to take him back into his mouth, Kenneth pulled his hair and tugged him to his feet. They pressed against each other, Kenneth's erection awkwardly pinned between their bodies, and kissed each other. Kenneth walked Simon back as he reached down to undo the other man's pants. He himself was partially hobbled, his boots holding his lowered pants around his calves, but they didn't have to go far.

Simon rested against the wall as Kenneth pulled his cock out and looked down at it. Short and thick, curving slightly to the left, the shaft looking slightly darker than the pink head. He was uncircumcised, the first Kenneth had ever seen, and he brushed his head over the foreskin to watch the shaft twitch in response. With a sigh, he angled his hips so they were resting against each other and he closed his hands around both. Simon's expert attention and his own pre-come provided enough lubrication as he squeezed, and they kissed again as they began thrusting against each other.

"Does that feel good?" Kenneth grunted.

Simon responded by wrinkling his nose and exhaling sharply. His face was shining in the moonlight, but his eyes were dark and heavy-lidded. He covered Kenneth's hand with his own so they were both stroking, then put his free hand on Kenneth's hip to guide his thrusts.

"You're going to have to say something, wolf." Kenneth was breathless. Sweat dripped down either side of his face. "I like to hear my lover's voice."

"Maybe your lovers should just shut up and fuck you."

Kenneth smiled, his teeth flashing in the darkness. "That's what you've wanted since we met, isn't it? You've wanted to fuck me. Here's your chance." He leaned close and swept his tongue over Simon's cheek, tasting him, scenting him, and growling low in his throat. "If you want it, fuckin' take it."

Simon let go of Kenneth and shoved him away. Kenneth stumbled over the pants wrapped around his legs and watched as Simon began tearing his clothes off. Kenneth did the same, awkwardly pulling off his boots and then finally freeing himself from the pants and underwear that had been inhibiting his motions. Simon nearly ripped his shirt in his haste to get it off.

Already naked, Kenneth idly stroked himself as he admired Kenneth's body. All the times they'd seen each other pre- and post-transformation didn't count. All wolves got used to seeing their friends and pack mates naked. Nudity only counted when there was arousal and attracted, when the reek of sex was thick in the air and made it an undeniably erotic situation. He was broad in the chest, narrow at the waist, and his pecs were covered in a thick layer of dark hair. His cock was fully erect and swung with his movements. It shone in the moonlight and would have drawn Kenneth's attention even if it wasn't the focus of his desire. His ears and cheeks burned as he kicked Simon's discarded clothes out of the way.

"What are you going to do?" Kenneth asked.

Simon stepped away from the wall and put his hand on Kenneth's shoulder. He pushed him forward, face against the wood, and pressed against him from behind.

"Say it, Loupin."

Simon kept his hand tight on Kenneth's shoulder. "I'm going to fuck you, Lieutenant."

Kenneth smiled and moved his feet apart. He felt Simon's cock pressing against his ass and closed his eyes in anticipation. Simon put his arms around Kenneth's waist and ran one hand up over his smooth stomach, scratching the skin with his fingernails before he gripped Kenneth in his hand to stroke him. Kenneth groaned and rapped his head against the wall. He felt like he was about to burst. The entire length of his erection was tingling, and each brush of Simon's hand against his tip was sheer torture. He was trembling and extremely aware of Simon hesitating.

"For God's sake, Simon, just fuck me already."

Simon pushed into him as soon as the words were out of Kenneth's mouth. Kenneth arched his back and flattened his palms against the wall. He pressed back as Simon stroked his cock, squeezing the base to hold off orgasm before moving his hand up to brush the head and bring Kenneth even closer to the edge. Simon moved closer to Kenneth's ear.

"You're not going to come until I tell you."

"You're making it difficult to follow your orders..."

Simon growled and lowered his head. He bit down on Kenneth's neck hard enough to hurt, but not enough to draw blood. Kenneth moaned and reached back, sliding his hand over Simon's flank. Simon pressed his hips tight against the curve of Kenneth's ass and squeezed the shaft of his cock. Kenneth dropped his head low, his free hand still against the wall with the fingers curling against the aged wood as he fought his climax, everything in him focused on the effort.

"Hurry. Goddamn it..."

Simon laughed and pressed tight against Kenneth, biting down on his cry of release so that it sounded like a roar of pain. His hand released Kenneth's erection and moved to his hips, holding him in place. Kenneth tensed when Simon's cock throbbed inside of him and, a moment later, he felt the other man's release. Simon muttered incoherently and slid his hands up Kenneth's bare back. Kenneth twisted away from him. His cock was painfully hard and it twitched with the effort of holding back his orgasm.

Without saying a word, Simon dropped to his knees and took it into his mouth again. The moment he felt Simon's lips around him, Kenneth came. He gasped Simon's name, hands in the other man's hair, hips thrusting of their own accord as Simon cupped and massaged his balls. Simon continued to slide his lips up and down Kenneth's length, teasing the sensitive shaft into spilling more come onto his tongue until he was spent.

Simon got to his feet and rested his forehead against Kenneth's, both men panting as they tried to catch their breath.

"Are you all right?" Kenneth asked.

"Yes." He cleared his throat and cupped the back of Kenneth's head. "What now?"

Kenneth said, "Now we sleep. If you wake up in the night and find me on top of you..."

Simon growled and made a fist in Kenneth's hair. "That would not go unappreciated."

Below them, the barn door scraped and protested as it was pushed open. Neither man reacted to the sound, knowing from instinct that it was either Min or Sandrine. A few seconds later, a wolf howled at the moon. The sound made Simon's hair stand on end, and he and Kenneth both looked toward the open loft door. They had just moved closer so they could see the ground when a second wolf took up the song. Sandrine and Min, in their wolf forms, were tilting their heads back to let loose a powerful and echoing howl.

Simon thought about Ulrich and the other Germans, demons in grey uniforms who had certainly discovered their comrade's mutilated corpse by that point. He imagined them in their beds, thinking about the wolf that had been in their midst earlier in the day. He could almost see their terrified eyes as the howling reached them. He glanced at Kenneth and without a word, both men transformed as well. They dropped into a crouch and stood in the open loft door.

The men added their voices to the howl, lifting its volume until it was certain to be heard by the squadron of assassins hiding in the factory. It became a chorus howl, one of them tapering off to take a breath while the others carried on. The night air filled with the sound until every other animal fell silent out of respect and, Simon was certain, every Nazi in the camp was checking out their windows to make sure they weren't being hunted.

CHAPTER NINETEEN

SIMON ANTICIPATED being confused when he woke. He expected Kenneth to be spooning him, to feel a strong arm on his thigh and think it was Philip. His fears were unfounded as he woke alone, lying on his side with his arms and legs stretched out in front of him. He'd gone to sleep in the wolf form and woke up having transformed in his sleep. He stretched out his limbs and arched his back before he scanned the loft for Kenneth.

He was standing at the barn door, naked and gilded by the early morning light. Simon rolled onto his hands and crawled across the loft. He remembered fucking as the wolf during the night, having Kenneth's wolf mount him and biting his neck. He also remembered Min and Sandrine being present for it, seeing them watch Kenneth fuck him. He stood up and wrapped his arms around Kenneth's waist. His morning erection pressed insistently against the curve of his new lover's ass.

"Good morning." He kissed the curve of Kenneth's neck. "Any sign of our compatriots?"

Kenneth said, "Not yet." He craned his neck to press his lips to Simon's temple. Simon tilted his head and their mouths met as Kenneth turned fully so they could embrace one another.

Sandrine cleared her throat from the ladder. "Gentlemen.

Perhaps we should be preparing for the big day we have."

Simon pecked Kenneth's bottom lip before stepping away from him. "She is not wrong. We have much to do."

Kenneth looked outside once more. "Yes," he agreed. "We do."

There was something off about him, something in his tone, but Simon decided not to pursue it at the moment. They had larger problems to take care of. He gathered his clothes and they both dressed, then climbed down the ladder to join the women by the car. Min was sitting on the hood in a pair of oversized trousers and an unbuttoned shirt. Her cheeks and ears burned red when she saw the men, but she was grinning from ear to ear. Kenneth offered her a wink and she chuckled shyly. Sandrine was stationed by the door. It stood open just a crack so she could see the road.

Min gestured at the rations she had set out. "Two portions for everyone. Sandrine said it was okay. I figure we'll be needing our strength."

Simon nodded. "Good thinking. While we're waiting for the others, I'll draw up a map of the factory as I remember it."

"Shouldn't you have done that immediately upon your return?"

"No," Simon said. "You know how the wolf mind tends to jumble things. I needed to sleep on it to let the information settle."

Sandrine said, "Oh, so you *did* get some sleep last night."

Simon bared his teeth at her, and she offered the smallest of smiles in return. They settled in to eat their breakfast in companionable silence. When he finished eating, Kenneth relieved Sandrine so she could eat as well. He put his shoulder against the wall and stared outside with a look of consternation and worry. Simon watched him until he couldn't bear it any longer.

"What is wrong with you? Is it about what happened last night?"

Kenneth shook his head. "No. That was phenomenal." His voice was muted, distracted, and he was still looking outside. "My concern is something far more pressing. Something has gone wrong."

Sandrine's defenses immediately clicked on. Her posture straightened and she locked her gaze on Kenneth.

"How so?" Simon said.

"They should be here. Giving Leopold and Irene time to reach Meldeuses, then inform everyone of what we've learned, gather supplies, and then head out, they should still have arrived by now. It's fifty kilometers. Even if they needed time to put together an armory, wouldn't your people have sent a few wolves ahead as soon as they were told about the situation?"

Simon was standing now. "Absolutely they would. Sending a few early would also prevent a mass migration. A few should have left immediately and the more prepared group would leave later. Presumably under cover of darkness."

Kenneth nodded. "Precisely my concern. Not only should they have arrived by now, we should by this time of day be greeting the final contingent. This barn should be overflowing with wolves. And yet, here we sit, completely alone."

Sandrine said, "This is very bad."

"It's potentially devastating," Kenneth said.

"We can still contact Chauny," Simon said. "Tell Didier and Jasper we need them to provide support. It might take them some time to get ready, but it's marginally closer than Meldeuses. We can be back here by this afternoon and take out the camp then."

Kenneth shook his head. "Those children aren't ready for a mission of this magnitude. But it gets worse."

"How could it get worse?" Min asked, her voice tremulous.

Kenneth crossed his arms and faced into the room. "If our people from Meldeuses aren't here, then we were right to worry about the mole. He or she obviously prevented Leopold and Irene from warning our friends. Everyone in Meldeuses may be lost to us."

Simon cursed under his breath.

"And our plans have been compromised. The mole knows where we are and what we plan to do. If we don't act now, Ulrich may be able to bolster his resources. Twelve hours from now that camp could have two hundred soldiers guarding every corner of it. We have to make a decision."

"What choice is there?" Sandrine said. "Either we abort, or the four of us try to take it out ourselves. One is a defeat and the other is suicide."

Kenneth said, "As distasteful as it is, those are the only options we have."

Min stood up, her good humor and flushed cheeks giving way to an ashen expression of doom. "Maybe they just needed time to gather weapons a-and supplies. Maybe they had to take a different route so they wouldn't attract suspicion. This barn isn't exactly easy to find. That's the point, right? That we don't stand out? They're probably just trying to find us without being conspicuous."

Simon said, "They wouldn't take this long to send out the first envoy. And if any member of the Loupin cell was looking for us, they would smell me and Simon from a mile away. That's why we never set up a rendezvous point. Wolves don't need one."

Sandrine was staring at Kenneth. "The truth is, we don't know what happened in Meldeuses. Only that our people are not here when they should be."

Kenneth nodded. "We learned in Chauny that the Germans have a mole in the resistance. As much as I hate to admit it, that mole is either in the Meldeuses cell or your pack."

"Or he's in this barn," Sandrine said.

For a moment, no one breathed. Simon looked at Sandrine and then at Kenneth. "What are you suggesting?"

Sandrine stepped closer to the Brit. "We only have his word about everything he's said. His entire identity could be a lie."

"He's a wolf," Simon said.

"Wolves have fought other wolves in the past," Sandrine said. "Mackay knew everything we know. He could have sent word to his superiors at any point. And now he's urging us to go on a suicide mission into Ulrich's stronghold? He's trying to get us killed. Don't let yourself be blinded to the obvious just because you fucked him last night."

Simon glared at her. Sandrine returned his look with just as much fury. "Who is being blinded here? We hardly know Kenneth, but we've known him longer than Minuit here."

The girl flinched as if she'd been hit.

Kenneth stepped forward. "And I led you to Isles-les-Meldeuses, so obviously we are working together. I set you up to meet Min here so we could end up in just this predicament. It's all very diabolical." He took his gun from its holster, gripped it by the barrel, and held it out to Sandrine. "No offense, Simon, but I feel like she would make it painless. Kill with the first bullet, the all-important head shot. If you truly believe I'm working with the Nazis, then pull the trigger."

Sandrine took the gun.

Min shrieked, "No! Please. No one here is working with the Nazis!"

Kenneth said, "I'm afraid they won't take you at your word, Minuit. After me, you're the prime suspect." He still hadn't taken his eyes off Sandrine, and he was still holding out the gun. "You can either trust me or shoot me. But then you'll have to shoot Min as well. Then you and Simon can accept defeat and return to Paris. I'm sure there's a bar he hasn't drunk dry yet."

Simon said, "That wasn't necessary."

"Your second-in-command is calling me a Nazi sympathizer. Forgive me if I'm not prepared to play polite."

Simon stepped forward and took the gun from Kenneth. "No one is killing anyone. Sandrine, you are letting your fear get the better of you. It's not an emotion you recognize, so you label it suspicion. But you know the truth. You know yourself and you know me. Would I have had sex with this man if I didn't trust him? Would you have taken Minuit under your wing if you had any doubts about her loyalty? We just learned something seriously terrifying. You're reacting to that and not the facts. What he's suggesting may be suicide, but it's also our only viable option. We can't wait to see if Ulrich increases his security. We have to take what little advantage we have to stop this camp from being brought to life. If you don't want to be part of this group, you can leave right now. None of us will think less of you."

Sandrine worked her jaw and finally looked away from them. "I don't want to die."

"I understand."

"But I also don't want to have a meaningless death. Of course I will stand beside you." She looked up at Kenneth again. "And you as well, if you're still willing."

Kenneth nodded. "Your reaction was understandable, given the circumstances. It's better to air our concerns now than in the heat of battle." He looked at the group. "Any other grievances?

Anything we should debate?"

Simon shook his head. Min pushed her hands into her hair and walked away toward the car. She hadn't made a noise, but it was obvious to Simon she was crying. Sandrine watched her pace and, after a moment, walked over to speak softly to her. At first the girl cringed away from Sandrine's touch but allowed an embrace after a few seconds.

Kenneth said, "Would she really have shot me?"

"Yes."

"Good. I've never served with anyone like her. It will be good to have her with us."

Simon nodded. The day had just become much grimmer, and their chances of seeing another sunset had dwindled to almost nil. But if he had to go on a mission that was almost certain to end with his death, there was no other group of soldiers he'd rather have backing him up.

In some ways, their lack of allies made things easier. With only four soldiers, their battle plan became simplified. Their sparse ammunition became a surplus since they could only carry four guns. Simon had drawn a map of the grounds and let Sandrine come up with their battle plan. Simon and Kenneth would enter the fence where Simon gained access the day before. Min would be on the road keeping watch for anyone entering or leaving the compound. She assured them she would be comfortable shooting at real people, despite having never done it before.

Sandrine gave her a gun. "If you can't bring yourself to kill, shoot out their tires. Aim to disable their vehicles, and then aim for their feet. Once they start shooting back, you'll lose any qualms you might have had."

"When do we attack?" Kenneth asked.

"We'll leave now and watch the compound from the forest until midday. They'll either be sitting down to a meal, or they'll be hungry."

Min said, "Or they'll have already eaten and will be sluggish."

Simon nodded. "Precisely. We'll go in as wolves, carrying our weapons and clothes with us in satchels. Even with the soldier I killed, they will be far slower to shoot an animal than they would a person. We can use that to our advantage." He looked down at his weapon. He could almost hear Philip's voice in his head giving some sort of inspirational speech, but the words wouldn't come. "This morning we were at one another's throats. We were suspicious and wary of the people standing beside us. That ends right now. We only have each other today. You all have three lives depending on you, and a thousand more who will be endangered if we fail. I have faith in all of you."

Sandrine held out her hand to Kenneth. He clasped her forearm and she gripped his. Whatever had passed between them during the argument earlier was put aside for the time being.

They loaded up their satchels with what they would need for the assault. Simon, Kenneth, and Min undressed and transformed into their wolves, then stood patiently while Sandrine fitted the satchels onto their bodies. The back of the satchel had a harness for their weapons, and Sandrine carefully secured the rifles along their spines. Min shifted a bit so the butt of her rifle was resting against her neck like a yoke. Min would carry Sandrine's supplies, since she wouldn't be able to get into a satchel as the wolf.

Once they were ready to go, the three wolves went outside. Sandrine followed them and secured the barn door before she stripped down and quickly transformed. Simon took off running toward the trees with Kenneth close on his heels and Min behind him. Once Sandrine shook her fur loose she brought up the rear.

Their wolves were well aware of what was being asked of them. There was a mission ahead, a goal, and they couldn't give in to their primal side. But being in the forest, with its multitudes of smells and distractions, brought out their wildness. Sandrine caught up to Min and barreled against the younger wolf's side. Min yapped in response and closed her teeth on Sandrine's tail. Simon and Kenneth were almost neck and neck when Kenneth leaned over and snapped his jaws at Simon's face. Simon responded by half-tackling the British wolf.

They were all hyper-aware of the weapons on their backs, but the wolves' delight in running free couldn't be contained. They were building up levels of adrenalin which would serve them well when they began the assault.

Simon brought them all to a halt at the tree line above the

camp. From their position they could only see a long length of blank gray wall broken by two iron doors and a section of iron bars. They were high enough to see the red clay roofs of the buildings just beyond the fence. Kenneth started down the incline, but Simon whined and nipped at his neck to stop him. It took Kenneth a moment to spot why, but he finally noticed the arch of silver metal rising from a freshly-turned pile of dirt next to the fence.

The Germans had set out wolf traps.

It would be impossible to know how many there were. They'd gotten lucky the one they saw was so haphazardly buried. Simon scanned the ground for evidence of any others in the area, but he wasn't going to risk his leg or the legs of his team. He nodded for Kenneth to follow him and cautiously went down the hill. When they reached the base of the slope, both sank onto their bellies and put their heads on the ground. They were looking for unusual mounds of dirt, clumps of grass or moss that seemed out of place, but they were also scenting the air. The Germans would try to conceal their human scent from the traps. Their attempts would hopefully flag each landmine.

Kenneth found the first one. He dug his forepaws in and pulled up the soft earth until a silver spring was exposed. He slid his paw under the sinister teeth and set it off. The snap was still startling enough that both Kenneth and Simon recoiled from it. They moved on to find the next trap, moving faster now that they knew what to look for. Only once did either of them come close to getting caught. Simon wasn't careful enough digging out one of the traps and it snapped before he was ready. It only cost him a few hairs on his front leg, but it was enough to ensure he was especially cautious on the next one.

While they were clearing the way, Sandrine moved down and slipped through the fence. They couldn't afford to lose reconnaissance time. She didn't clear the change of plan with Simon, but they'd worked together long enough for her to know he would agree to it if she had. She wriggled through the fence and kept close to the building until she reached the mouth of the alley. A quick glance around the corner of the building revealed a German soldier was standing guard.

He was young and inexperienced, but that meant he was taking his duty seriously. He was standing almost at attention with his rifle held across his midsection, eyes forward and chin up. She knew he would only lose focus under the most extreme circumstances. She backed away from the corner and rocked back onto her haunches. She stood up as she transformed, wobbling a bit on her back paws before they stretched out into feet. She flexed her toes and popped her shoulders. She held her breath for thirty seconds, just long enough to gasp as she lurched around the corner.

"Help me," she panted.

He brought his gun up as he swung toward her, but the barrel was instantly lowered when he saw that she was naked. She put her hand against the wall and swayed backward out of sight.

"*Fraulein?*" He came around the corner still holding his rifle, but it was by his side. Sandrine grabbed his throat and swung him around to slam him against the wall. He tried to raise his rifle but there was no angle for him to hit her. She pulled the gun away with her free hand. Her thumb and forefinger stretched over his windpipe. She stood on the balls of her feet and leaned against him with all her strength. His eyes were terrified, wide open and full of bursting blood vessels as he clawed at her. Sandrine didn't blink or let up until she felt his throat give under her hand.

The soldier fell. Sandrine looked to make sure no one had approached in the past few seconds, then crouched to strip off his uniform. He was a young man, barely out of his teens, so his clothes would fit her well enough. She would do her best to keep anyone from getting close enough to examine her closely. If anyone did, she would just dispatch them as well. She looked at the nametag and identified herself as *Leutnant* Graf.

She pulled on the man's clothes, put on his helmet, then took his wrists and dragged him closer to the fence. There was a thin area behind the building where his body would hopefully go unnoticed long enough for her to disappear into the compound. She put him on his back and folded his legs up, tucking him in as if he was cowering from the cold.

When she straightened up, she saw Simon watching from the other side of the fence. He nodded to her, and she winked at him with a smile. He darted off to continue his mission. Sandrine checked her surroundings once more, smoothed down the front of her stolen jacket, and went off to find someone else to kill.

CHAPTER TWENTY

"WOLF! WOLF *im Lager!*"

Two enlisted men came running at the cry, already on alert due to their friend's death the day before. The man in the lead pointed to where the voice had come from and rounded the corner with his gun drawn. He barely had time to register the alley or the slender officer standing against the wall before the sharp edge of a knife was dragged across his throat. The soldier withdrew her knife and stepped out, bringing her gun up from her hip to shoot the second soldier in the head. She emerged from concealment to pull her victims out of sight, tucking them against the fence before jogging away.

"*Wolf im Lager!*"

The call was being echoed now. Sandrine could hear boots on concrete as soldiers responded to the hue and cry. She kept the knife in her hand, blade out and facing forward so she could slice as she threw a punch. The first group she saw had their gaze lowered, watching the ground for anything on four legs, so her uniform was enough of a disguise to get her close enough to dispatch them. A knife to the first soldier. Shooting left-handed at the one behind him and then sweeping gunfire at the space behind him to take out anyone else.

Five Germans were dead and at least two more were injured. She could hear them jabbering at one another and assumed her ruse was being exposed. She didn't care. She kept her helmet on so it would make it harder to tell friend from foe. When she reached the next intersection she pressed hard against the wall and listened to the sound of approaching boots. Two men ran past her and she shot them both in the back of the head, just below their helmets.

As they fell, the air filled with another chorus howl. She heard Kenneth, then Simon, and a fraction of a second later, Min joined them. Kenneth tapered off to take a breath and resumed louder than before. Min whooped and yipped before starting a new, lower cry. Their howls echoed off the stone of the camp until it was impossible to tell what direction they came from and exactly how many wolves there were. The entire base sounded as if it was surrounded.

She stepped around the corner of the building and was shoved from behind, knocked off her feet and flat onto her stomach. She didn't hear the echo of the gunshot until she rolled over and felt the blood pouring over her skin beneath her jacket. Her left shoulder throbbed with pain as she looked up at a red-faced German, focusing on the vein above his right eyebrow as he leveled a gun at her head.

"*Franzosisch hund,*" he growled.

Sandrine swung her gun up and pulled the trigger at the same time the German pulled his.

Kenneth disabled what he believed to be the last wolf trap as the camp filled with shouting and the sound of gunfire. The satchels were designed to be loosened by a strap that hung near the wolf's right shoulder. He grabbed it with his teeth, pulled, and shimmied out of the material so he wouldn't be weighted down with supplies.

He pushed through the fence and took off at a dead run. The entire area reeked of blood and the dehumanizing odors of death, so he was able to follow Sandrine's trail of destruction through the camp. He rounded a corner and saw two Germans lying side by side still alive, still clutching their wounds, but he stopped when he recognized the stench of one. He moved close to Sandrine's side. He whimpered when he saw the entire left side of her uniform blouse covered in thick black blood. Her face was pale and mottled with ruby-red droplets.

"Go," she gasped, lips trembling. "Get out of here. Finish the job."

He looked at the man who had shot her. She'd apparently hit him in the throat, and his last breath was fighting with his blood to escape the jagged wound. Kenneth thought about ending the struggle but decided the man deserved a slow death. He nudged Sandrine's hand with his snout.

"Get out of here. Goddamn Brit..."

He gave her hand one final nudge, spotted her knife, and took it in his teeth. It tasted of her sweat and smelled of blood, which in his mind would make whatever he did with it Sandrine's victory. She nodded to him and he turned away to leave her.

Simon's map had shown trucks on the southern wall, near the main gate. He ran to them with the knife clamped tightly in his jaw. A soldier spotted him and shouted before opening fire. Kenneth felt the breeze as several rounds barely missed him, but as far as he could tell he wasn't hit. He evaded them through the maze of buildings and ducked underneath the fence surrounding their motor pool. The air filled with German shouts that grew closer and closer to his location, but he was focused on his task.

With the blade held tightly in his mouth, he crawled under the first truck and twisted his neck to sever the fuel line. Gasoline began pouring out onto his paws and the pavement, and he breathed a sigh of relief. An intelligence report he'd happened to glance at indicated the Germans were devoting all their diesel fuel to the panzer divisions, leaving gasoline for their vehicles on the continent. His plan wouldn't have worked with diesel in the trucks, and he crawled through the growing wall of fumes to the next vehicle.

For once, his heightened senses were a liability. It became harder to breathe and see with every line he cut, but he pushed forward. He knew where the lines were on each truck so he could do it with his eyes closed if need be. The soldiers were surrounding the motor pool now. He cut the final line and hunkered under the truck's frame until the coast was mostly clear. His heart pounded and a prayer filled his mind as he broke out into the open and dashed for the fence.

His plan required one or more of the Germans to fire on him. He got his wish just before reaching the fence. He crouched to leap, the sound of a rifle cracked the air, and the explosion of gunpowder ignited the fumes. The explosion was literally deafening; Kenneth heard an impossibly loud snap just before it was drowned out by an all-consuming whistle. His muscles pushed him into the air, and the force of the explosion carried him forward. His head cracked against the fence and he tumbled, falling hard to the concrete.

He struggled to get up, but his senses were under assault. His nose burned, the ringing had faded to a terrifying nothingness, and his vision had been diminished by dark curtains closing in on all sides. He managed a few shaky steps before his legs gave out, dumping him back to the ground. The darkness pulled in tighter, and he closed his eyes so he wouldn't have to see the German who finished the job.

Min's body tensed with every gunshot. She knew there couldn't be more than a dozen, maybe twenty, soldiers in the camp, but at the moment it sounded like hundreds of them were shouting. At one point she heard Sandrine shouting in German. Crouching outside the camp, well away from any danger, Min continued scolding her cowardice. She knew Sandrine and Simon had put her here because it was the wisest course of action. She was the least experienced of them all, she was wary about using deadly force, and she wasn't brave enough to hide her fear about going into the camp.

She was wearing Sandrine's jacket because it smelled like her. She was wearing Simon's pants and Kenneth's shirt. Her cell in Meldeuses were the people she'd grown up with. They were people she had known all her life. But now, in the space of a week, she had a whole new family. She loved them all more than she would've thought possible. She loved Sandrine fiercely. The thought of them being in danger while she sat safely in the woods was making her queasy.

The road was completely empty in both directions. She wondered how vital her role was, if standing guard was truly a necessary task or if it had just been designed to keep her out of the way. It didn't take her long to decide it didn't matter. Four people taking on an entire camp was suicide, but they were trying to do it with three. She took off her pack and slipped a revolver into her belt, picked up her rifle, and stood up to join the fray.

Min had just stood up when something inside the camp exploded. She was so startled that she fell backward onto her ass, staring in horror at the fireball rising above the now-broken camp wall. It looked as if a truck had been thrown against the wall hard enough to leave a crevasse behind, dust still falling from the unbelievable wound. Men were screaming in agony and she could feel the heat from the flames even from where she sat. Her hands were shaking and her eyes were dry from not blinking. The fire was as gorgeous as it was terrible, and she felt bile at the back of her throat for thinking something so deadly was also beautiful.

Min could almost hear Sandrine telling her to get off her ass, so she did it. She stood, checked to make sure she had her weapons, and then started down the hill at a run. Flaming debris had fallen on the grass outside the walls and she stepped around it to crawl through the new opening created by the explosion. The heat on the other side was almost unbearable. Simon and Kenneth said the factory was designed to prevent fire from spreading, but it also did a commendable job keeping it contained.

The few seconds she spent skirting the fire was enough to inhale enough smoke to make her cough. She could feel ash and soot on her face as she climbed over a misshapen fence and moved forward. She tripped over something warm and soft and aimed her gun at it before she recognized it was a wolf. There was blood coming from its ears and from a nasty gash on top of its head. It wasn't moving and, with the smoke and tears in her eyes, it was hard to tell if it was breathing at all.

She dropped next to him, recognizing it as Kenneth as she pulled his head onto her lap. "Please be alive," she said. "Please... please..."

"*Legen sie ihre waffen!*"

Min bared her teeth and spun toward the voice. The German had lost his helmet, dark blonde hair sticking up in spikes above a soot-darkened face. He was aiming a rifle at her. Min put down Kenneth's head and gave a wordless cry of fury as she brought up her weapon. He reached for the trigger but Min pulled hers first. A streak of blood splashed across his forehead and he went down hard. Min felt fresh tears burning her eyes as she got to her feet and moved closer to see if he was dead. She was almost to his body when someone pressed against her from behind and slashed at her throat with his knife.

Sandrine's coat, so large for her frame that there was ample material piled at her throat to catch the blade. She slapped his hand away, turned, and threw her weight against him. He kept his grip on the knife and pushed it into the folds of her coat. She felt its sharp edge running along her side, but she didn't know if it had broken the skin. She put her leg between his, hooked her foot on his ankle, and pulled. He took her down with him and she used his bulk to break her fall.

She lifted up to continue her attack, but someone grabbed the collar of her jacket and hauled her up off his body. She was thrown against the wall and hit the ground hard, dazed and disoriented so she couldn't defend herself when her attacker sat on her. She tried to protect her face, but it was no use. He punched her once so hard that she thought she heard bells. He hit her again and she felt her teeth tearing her bottom lip open. The third hit was hard enough that she passed out, so anything afterward was blissfully unfelt.

CHAPTER TWENTY-ONE

SIMON APPLAUDED Sandrine's decision to enter the camp even before he saw evidence of the destruction she was causing. He could discern at least five dead bodies, maybe more, as he moved through the camp. Sandrine and Kenneth had entered from the west, so he skirted the camp to scramble over its eastern wall. Shouting and gunfire grew fainter as soldiers responded to the incursion, and he met no resistance as he moved between the buildings toward Ulrich's stronghold in the center of the compound.

A soldier appeared ahead of him, so focused on the sounds of combat that he didn't see Simon. The split second of distraction was all Simon needed. He lunged at the soldier and sank his teeth into the man's dominant arm. When he pulled free, he had a mouthful of blood and cloth. The soldier was young and green enough that his instincts took over his training. He swung his rifle like a bat instead of shooting, and Simon easily ducked it. He threw himself at the boy's waist and knocked him over. The boy dropped his gun and clawed at Simon's face, but he couldn't dig his nails in because of the fur.

The boy had been shrieking in barely intelligible German from the moment Simon bit him. The smell of clove and urine alerted him to the second soldier's arrival, and he rolled to one side at the very last moment. The other soldier's knife missed Simon's head and sank into the chest of the man he was trying to save. Simon flipped onto his feet. The knife-wielder was fortunately much older than the boy he'd just killed, and Simon didn't hesitate to go for this throat.

He left the two soldiers where they fell. He had just started running again when the entire world seemed to be picked up and shaken. The shock of the explosion knocked Simon off his feet, and he could hear the volume of shouts increase as everyone rushed toward the sound. He continued forward knowing that Ulrich would stay in the safety of his office even as the rest of the base swarmed the attackers. He would certainly have guards, but hopefully they could be easily dispatched.

Someone behind him opened fire and he did his best to dodge and duck the bullets. They skipped and sparked off the concrete in front of him but he didn't think he was hit as he rounded the corner. He spotted Ulrich's building directly ahead. Even above the clamor of warfare he could hear his own breath and the clack of his nails on the concrete as he ran.

He saw a flash of gray cloth to his right and darted out of its way, but the soldier wasn't carrying a knife or gun. He tossed something metal at the ground ahead of Simon. It was trailing a chain and clanked loudly as it landed. Simon had less than a second to identify it as a wolf trap and change direction. He skidded onto his side, but it was too late. His back foot triggered the mechanism and it snapped shut on his right leg.

The pain was unimaginable. He felt as if his leg was cut off at the impact point, but he could feel the pain radiating through his entire leg. He couldn't stand, couldn't walk, could barely think through the agony. The soldier put a knee on Simon's chest to keep him from breathing in and held his head against the ground. Simon tried to pull free, but each time his body twisted sent the blades deeper into his leg. The soldier had a knife, and he angled it toward Simon's throat.

Simon didn't trigger the change, nor was he consciously aware of it, but when he lashed out with his forepaw it was a human fist that struck his attacker. He rolled onto his back, the chain of the wolf trap clanking on the ground as he threw the soldier off. His transformation was smooth until it came to his back leg. The blades had snapped shut around a thin wolf leg, and his human leg was twisted and further mangled by its grip. Tears streamed down his face as he reached down and forced the jaws open, pulled his blood-soaked foot free, and then let it snap shut again.

The German stared at him in shock and horror, jaw trembling as he tried to retreat from the naked and angry man now looming over him. Simon couldn't put any weight on his right leg, which had become numb from the knee down. He fell onto the German and took the knife from him. He stabbed, jabbed, sliced, and ripped until his entire torso was covered with blood. Only then did he pull back and sink the knife into the soldier's heart.

He fell onto his side and looked down at his leg. An entire chunk was missing on either side of his leg, and he felt as if the bone had been shattered. Whether it was from the initial impact of the trap or transforming with it still on his leg, the pertinent fact was that he had just been hobbled. His hands were trembling and he felt cold all over even though he was dripping sweat. He looked at the dead German beside him and took the time to peel off his blood-soaked uniform. He used it to cover his own nudity and painfully got up, leaning against the wall.

He could flee. He was a liability now, dead weight that would only slow them down. He could only hope the others had been more successful and that he could get out of the camp without being caught. He looked for the wall, an indication of how far he would have to go before reaching relative safety, but then he saw something that shattered his plans of retreat.

A German soldier was carrying something toward Ulrich's office. A person, limp and obviously unconscious, was draped across his arms. She looked unbelievably tiny, but there was no doubt that the body was Minuit. There was blood in her hair, enough that it had been transferred onto the soldier's uniform. Simon leaned down and retrieved the dead soldier's gun and knife. The rifle was long enough for him to use it as a crutch. He couldn't move fast, but he could move.

The soldier carrying Min was already inside by the time Simon reached the door. He was drenched with sweat, aching everywhere, but he pulled the door open and went inside. A trail of blood followed him across the hardwood floor. He heard voices in the inner office and walked in as confidently as he could muster.

The soldier had dropped Min on the ground like she was a sack of potatoes. His back was to the door and Ulrich didn't get a chance to warn him as Simon brought up the pistol and shot him in the back of the head. Ulrich had been leaning against the desk and leapt to his feet as his man fell. The *Oberst*'s eyes were wide behind his glasses as he regarded the feral beast of a man who was standing before him. Simon's chest was covered with the blood of the German who had crippled him, and he knew that his right leg was most likely completely red with his own blood.

The barrel of the gun shook as he tried to aim it at Ulrich. "Do not move. Hands to your sides at shoulder-length, *Herr* Ulrich."

Ulrich slowly complied. When he spoke, it was in accented French. "Are you responsible for this madness? My men tell me there are trained wolves at play. How on Earth—"

"Be quiet. Have you called for reinforcements?"

Ulrich stared at him.

"I asked you a question."

"I am aware." He looked at Min. "The girl is unfortunate. So young to be involved in such a futile endeavor. She could have had a good life."

Simon refused to take the bait. He kept his eyes on Ulrich, unwavering.

"Did you come here to kill me, wild man? Put a bullet in my head? You are more than welcome to pull the trigger and succeed. It would appear to be a Pyrrhic victory, however. I've been receiving reports for the past ten minutes. All of your companions are dead. The girl is hanging on... youth are so resilient. But unless she receives medical attention, I fear she won't bounce back from the beating my men gave her. And your leg? That much blood cannot be a good thing. Good God, man, you're standing in a lake."

Simon grit his teeth and glared at his foe. He couldn't be telling the truth. Sandrine and Kenneth had to still be alive. He would have felt it otherwise. He would have sensed the truth in Ulrich's words. As it was, his taunt fell hollow.

"Do you believe what you're doing here will mean anything? This camp was being built to house prisoners who are currently being packed together like sardines in buildings that cannot support them. They have no privacy, no room to breathe, no toilet. Do you think those people will thank you for taking this place away from them? This place where they will have beds and fresh air?"

"This place where you will herd them like animals and kill them in furnaces or gas chambers."

"There is no reason for them to be uncomfortable as they await their fates. It is, after all, only humane."

Simon growled. "Humane? You are demons. You are slaughtering countless~"

"How many men did you kill today?" He gestured at the corpse laying at Simon's feet. "Are you any different than us?"

"You murder innocent people. These are the men who chose to help you with that mission."

"So they deserve to die?"

"Yes."

Ulrich shrugged. "This girl chose to help you kill my men. Then I believe she deserves to die. She is staining my carpet as we speak... I shall always remember her. The French whore that sacrificed her life for no reason." He spit, and Simon tensed even though it didn't land anywhere near her body. "This was is bigger than one man or one camp. You destroy us here, we will build another elsewhere. You kill me, there are a thousand more just like me waiting to take my place. You cannot win."

"No. I cannot. I'm just one man. Minuit was only a woman. But people will see what happened here. They will see that four people stood up against evil, knowing they would lose, and they fought with everything they had to make that evil bow down. Others will take up our cause when we're gone. They will fight because they see how close we came. In the end, this is war is about beliefs. Your belief that you are stronger and better than everyone else. And our belief that the good in the world will always outweigh its evils. Today we might fall. But tomorrow this camp will be useless to your cohorts. It will not be used as a charnel house. That is our victory."

"You... almost sounded like Philip... for a moment."

Simon didn't take his eyes off Ulrich, but his heart lurched at the sound of Sandrine's voice. He could hear her hand sliding along the wall for support as she joined them in the office. He stepped to one side so he could see her in his peripheral vision. Her entire left side was covered with blood. She was aiming a pistol at Ulrich, but it was wavering so much he doubted any shot she made would actually find its mark. She leaned against the chair with a heavy groan.

"Minuit?"

"I believe she is alive."

"Kenneth?"

"I don't know."

Sandrine took a deep breath through her nose. "For what it's worth, I agree with you. Even if all four of us die, today will be a victory. Because it is a loss for these German devils."

Ulrich laughed. "Quite a formidable duo you make. Your right leg, her left... everything. Together you make one pathetic human being. Do your ears work? Because as I told you, I've been getting reports ever since your attack began. Where do you think those reports are coming from?"

The outer door of the building slammed open. Sandrine turned to face the door. Ulrich threw a paperweight from the desk at Simon. Simon stepped to one side to avoid the projectile and, in doing so, put weight on his right leg. He howled in pain and went down as Ulrich lunged at him.

Min sat up and wrapped her arms around Ulrich's thighs. He fell forward. Simon recovered in time to press his gun against Ulrich's throat and pull the trigger. The door opened and Sandrine shot the man who came through before he had time to register the carnage taking place within. Ulrich's body fell heavily to the rug, the back of his head a bloody ruin. A good portion of his blood had rained down on Min, who it seemed had fallen unconscious after her heroic act.

Sandrine fell onto the floor, clutching her side. Simon went down as well. The room smelled of gunpowder and blood, and Simon's ears rang from the gunshots. He rested his gun in his lap and closed his hands into fists to quell their shaking.

"Kenneth?" he asked.

"I did not see him." She coughed and whimpered softly. She put her hand against the hole in her jacket, her fingers already coated with her blood.

"How many more soldiers are outside?"

Sandrine shook her head. "Not many." She was breathing heavily, roughly, and it seemed difficult for her to inhale. She looked at Min. "If he called for reinforcements, we are sunk."

Simon threw his head back and laughed. "But if he didn't, we are absolutely fine."

Sandrine laughed as well. "Yes. Everything is perfect so long as there are not more soldiers coming. It is a beautiful day, in that case."

"He was right, you know."

"Perhaps. But so were you."

There were footsteps on the tile floor outside. "*Oberst? Was ist passiert?*" Simon brought his gun up. The soldier was cautious as he came around into the doorway, but he was focused on the far side of the room. Simon pulled the trigger and killed the man where he stood.

"Minus one," he said.

"Things are looking up." Sandrine sagged to one side and scooted across the carpet. Min was lying on her side next to Ulrich's body, and Sandrine propped herself against the small of the girl's back. She was still facing the door, and she aimed her rifle at the opening to take out whoever came through next.

"She's breathing," Sandrine reported.

Simon smiled. "As you said. Things are looking up."

They could still hear the fire raging outside, along with the occasional shout in German. Eventually someone would come to find Ulrich. Maybe they would come in force. Whatever happened, they would keep fighting until they won or they were eventually overwhelmed. Given their wounds, it was likely their war was over no matter what.

It would be good to go out in a grand fashion.

CHAPTER TWENTY-TWO

A PRETERNATURAL silence fell over the forest after the final gunshot sounded. In nearby Saint-Pierre-Aigle, constables assured townspeople that there was nothing to fear. They promised to go investigate the source of the explosions and gunfire, but it would be dark in an hour or two. No one was willing to be caught at that camp after dark. Answers could wait for morning. Until then, the townspeople could bolt their doors and windows and stay as quiet as possible.

Seven hours after the assault began, and two hours after the sounds of warfare died down, three trucks approached the ruins of the camp. Jasper was behind the wheel of the lead vehicle and he slowed down when he saw what awaited them. The fire was still burning. From where he came to a stop, he could see a fully-engulfed truck through the open gate. There were bodies scattered all around. Didier was sitting beside him in the passenger seat. The old man took a deep breath and let it out slowly, his eyes swimming with tears that he quickly wiped away.

He had feared this since leaving Chauny the morning before. Some instinct had warned him something was wrong, so he gathered Jasper's people and went to Meldeuses to reassure himself that the plan was running smoothly. What he found was a massacre in progress. Bijou, Ambrose, Ivonne, and Maxime were all dead. Gilles and Anatole were fighting in the pantry and each declared the other to be a traitor when Didier entered the room.

Didier looked at his pack mates, two men he would have laid down his life to protect, and saw two damning pieces of evidence: blood on Gilles' trousers and only defensive wounds on Anatole's hands. Didier killed Gilles without hesitation. Anatole revealed that Gilles made his true allegiances known that morning. He was their radio officer, and he'd been sending messages to the Germans since before Philip's death.

Didier was forced to make another impossible decision. He knew he should gather the pack and head out to help Simon, but he couldn't leave their people behind. They needed a proper burial. There was every chance they would be unable to return to the farmhouse, so it was their only opportunity to do right by their friends. He made the decision to honor their remains. Now it seemed that their funerals - rushed as they were - might have cost Simon, Kenneth, Sandrine, and Min their lives.

He pushed away the guilt and recriminations. "Let's go get our people."

Jasper rolled forward to block the entrance with his truck before they got out. Jasper was walking with a limp he'd acquired in Meldeuses, when they walked into the ambush at the farmhouse. He knew Didier was probably hurting even worse, but he wasn't letting it slow him down. The rest of the cell climbed out of the trucks and flanked out to make sure the camp had been successfully cleared. Didier tried to scent the air but immediately regretted the attempt. Gunpowder, smoke, dead bodies, and blood formed a fug over the camp that made tracking by smell impossible.

Jasper spotted something unusual a few yards away from the camp gate. "Didier. Is..." He gestured with his rifle. "Is that a naked person?"

"*Nique ta mere...*"

Didier ran over to where Kenneth was propped against the wall. His hair was matted from a gash on his right temple, and more blood had caked in his ears. The trail of blood indicated he had dragged himself almost ten feet to get where he ended up. Didier knelt next to him and Kenneth shot one hand out, weakly slapping his fingers against the other man's chest. Didier grabbed Kenneth's wrist and squeezed as he turned and shouted for Irene.

She ran to them, stepping over Kenneth's legs and gently holding his head up so she could see his eyes. "Kenneth? Look at me." He looked at her, but didn't seem to recognize her. He blinked, squinted, and then looked past her at the camp. Irene patted his cheek. "Kenneth? Kenneth, focus here, please…"

His head lolled forward but Irene and Didier kept him upright.

"Concussion," Irene said, "and probably hearing loss judging by the amount of blood in his ears. I'll take care of him. Go."

Didier's knees protested as he stood up and went in search of their other missing people. Someone shouted from a building near the center of the compound and Didier moved in a fast shuffle to see what had been found. The boy who'd cried out was stupidly young, one of Jasper's people from Chauny, and he rushed off to throw up as Didier pushed past him into the building. He immediately saw what had caused the boy to be sick: seven German soldiers were lying in a heap in the open door of an office, most of them missing part or all of their faces.

"*Merde…*" He tugged the collar of his T-shirt over his mouth and nose to dull the smell as he stepped over the pile of corpses and entered the room.

Simon was slumped against a chair that held the headless corpse of someone in a German officer's uniform. His right leg below the knee was almost too disgusting to look at, but it was clear he'd been gravely injured. Sandrine and Min were in the middle of the room. Her uniform was bloody, her complexion ashen, and it was an obvious struggle just to keep her eyes open.

Sandrine lowered her gun. "Announce yourself… next time… old man," she wheezed as she slumped back against Min. "I could've… added you to… the pile."

"I heard the clicking when you pulled the trigger on me. When did you run out of bullets?"

"Right after… I stopped needing them." She smiled weakly and gasped again. Each word seemed to require a feat of strength to get out. "My girl… is still breathing. Check on Simon."

Didier shuffled to one side. "Heartbeat. Breathing, but only just. I'll go get help."

As he stood to leave, Sandrine said, "Wait... Kenneth... We lost track of Kenneth."

"He's alive. Beat up as bad as you three, but he's alive."

Sandrine nodded. "Good. Looks... like a... win after all."

Didier looked at the three torn-up and chewed-out wolves lying in the office in front of him. "Heh. Victory looks strange in this war."

Sandrine smiled and sagged against the girl she was using as a pillow. Didier stepped around the bodies again and went to find someone to help him move his friends. The resistance members he'd brought with him had reconvened near the trucks, and he walked to join them.

"We need medics and anyone who doesn't get squeamish at the sight of blood. Our people are alive, but it took most everything they had. We need to get them stabilized and moved."

Several people volunteered immediately. Didier pointed them to where they needed to go, and Jasper stepped forward.

"My people tell me the base is clear. Nearly twenty German soldiers, all killed. Shot or burnt or beaten. Four people did this?"

"It might be hard to believe. But I know who the four people were. I know what the Nazis took from Simon." He looked at the destruction. "This looks about right."

Jasper still looked shocked. "What about the camp? The Nazis could still clean up this mess and turn it into a concentration camp."

Didier smiled. "You know one thing the Germans and I actually have in common? We both believe in the supernatural. We'll get Simon's team on your truck and your people can get them medical attention. Let my people take care of the camp."

Just before dawn, a fleet of German trucks rolled through Saint-Pierre-Aigle. *Hauptmann* Joseph von Meyer was in charge of the unit, bringing men and supplies to bring the new camp into operational order. He envisioned himself settling in under the command of *Oberst* Ulrich and then sending word to the nearby camps that they were ready for prisoners. He was tremendously at peace, knowing that soon he would be in charge of a camp full of people whose lives were in his hands. He could choose which of them would live, who would die and when, and he would have to answer to no one for his actions. Just the thought was enough to excite him. He could hardly wait to begin.

"*Ist dass rauch?*" the driver asked.

Meyer looked ahead and saw smoke rising from the trees. He was perturbed at the sight, assuming Ulrich had started the executions without him. He'd wanted to experience the first death personally. An untainted room transformed into a death chamber at the push of his finger. He would never admit it out loud, but the thought of the job ahead of him was highly arousing. He wet his lips at the thought of marching people into a furnace and—

"*Himmel, arsch und Zwirn!*" The driver stood on the brakes.

Meyer had to brace his hand against the dashboard to stop himself from going through the glass. There was enough room for the trucks behind them to stop without an accident, but the squeal of their brakes sounded like wounded animals in the forest he had just now noticed seemed unnaturally silent. He curled his hand into a fist to discipline the driver for his sudden stop, but then he saw what was ahead of them in the road. He couldn't form words for the sight, so he stared slack-jawed and tried to make sense of it.

Three rows of people were blocking the road, each row made up of officers lying shoulder-to-shoulder. Their skin was pale, their uniforms covered with blackened blood. Just beyond them was the camp, the source of the smoke they'd seen earlier. Everything was on fire. Within the stone walls, it looked as if someone had reached into the Earth and drawn up flames from the depths of hell.

Standing between the open gate and the gruesome display of corpses were wolves. Meyer counted eight, but smoke had made the air hazy. The beasts seemed to be standing in formation, eyes forward, ignoring the fire behind them and the corpses in front of them to stare at the trucks. He didn't know much about wolves, but he knew that this was *wrong*. It felt as if a block of ice had formed in the center of his chest as he stared at the animals.

And then they began to howl. Not one taking the lead with the others following him, but all eight or ten at once tilted their heads back and howled into the air. Meyer couldn't stop himself from shuddering at the sound of it, and the cab of the truck filled with a pungent odor as the driver released his bowels.

"*Ruckzug*," Meyer managed to choke out, ordering the retreat. When the driver didn't immediately comply, Meyer shouted the order. The young man put the vehicle in reverse and moved without thinking. They smashed against the front of the truck behind them.

The wolves began to advance.

"*Ruckzug!*" Meyer shrieked, leaning out the window. He waved for the other vehicles to reverse, watching as the animals slowly approached. Gears were grinding as the trucks tried to comply, but they were moving too slowly. He opened the door and dropped to the grass, his terror overwhelming his better judgment as he ran. The howl was unbearably loud now. It echoed through the trees. Or maybe those were other wolves, unseen in the shadows, waiting to pounce.

The final truck in their convoy was backing up at full speed, though the driver couldn't know why. Meyer looked back to see if the wolves were gaining on him and tripped over his own foot. He shrieked as he fell tumbling into the road. His right arm was crushed under the truck's tire first, giving him just enough time to feel an agony he'd never before experienced before it continued backward over his head.

His last thought was that no one, German or French, would ever dare set up camp on this accursed piece of ground.

EPILOGUE

THE WAR was over. Some mornings Simon Renaudin reminded himself of that fact immediately upon waiting. Sometimes he waited until breakfast or when he was out for a walk. The war was over and their side had won. France was free once more. Hitler was dead. The worst army that had ever terrorized Europe was defeated and crushed under the heels of a stronger force. It was still enough to bring a tear to his eye and a smile to his lips.

He was back in Paris after spending the past six months in London. The world felt changed in every way; from sunlight to the way people went about their day. The war left its scars on everyone. He reached under the table to massage the joint where his real leg met the prosthetic. He lost everything below the knee during an impromptu surgery on the road from Saint-Pierre-Aigle to Meldeuses. He only survived due to a transfusion of blood from Irene, who was also the one amputating his leg. Afterward he thanked her and called her his architect. She taught him who he was, and now she had changed his very shape.

She smiled and cupped his face, then left him to recover. Six months later she was shot and killed by a Nazi guard. Didier passed away in his sleep. A heart attack in the middle of a war zone. Simon's grief was tempered by how irritated Didier would have been to know how mundane his death ended up being. "We spend decades trying to matter," Kenneth had said, "and in the end, what we hope for is a quiet death in our beds."

He sat outside at the restaurant so he could watch passersby. Life went on. Streets that had once borne the weight of troop transports were now filled with people window-shopping or on their way to brunch. Shuttered businesses opened once again like flowers reviving after a long winter. The world was getting back to normal, and those like Simon who had sacrificed to make it happen were still trying to adjust.

Kenneth had lost most of the hearing in his left ear. He adjusted well, and he could hear most of what was said around him in a casual setting, but he didn't trust himself in combat. His superiors granted his request to remain in France with the Loupin pack where he remained in a support capacity for the remainder of the war. Simon also stayed off the frontlines, even when Sandrine joked he had taken over Didier's position as the resident grump. After everything he'd seen and done at Ulrich's camp, he was more than happy to leave the gunplay to younger recruits.

Min suffered worse than any of them. She struggled to sleep, and when she succeeded there was no true rest due to nightmares about what she'd seen and done. Her scars healed, but she still remembered the terror of being held down and beaten by the soldier, and she was conflicted about the part she'd played in Ulrich's death. She knew what she'd done was necessary. Simon had told her multiple times that her bravery was the only reason all four of them had survived the day. One morning Sandrine woke to find Min in the bathroom chopping off all her hair. Sandrine took the scissors from her and finished the hatchet job, then carefully shaved away the excess.

In time, she found a measure of peace in her relationship with Sandrine. As if summoned by his thoughts, the two women came around the corner at the end of the street. Simon chuckled under his breath when he saw Sandrine. The woman he'd known in the war no longer existed. In her place was a lithe and elegant French maiden, with long waves of curly hair and a smile that he didn't think her face was capable of supporting. She was still light on her feet, but watching her approach in high heels and a summer dress made it impossible to picture her carrying a rifle or emptying a clip at any German stupid enough to stick his head around a door frame.

He thought about how lucky they'd been that afternoon. The Nazis could have hurled a grenade into the office, they could have fired blindly through the window and ended the standoff in a flash. After much consideration he realized they must have believed Ulrich was still alive and capable of being rescued. Their blind hope was the only reason he, Sandrine, and Min had survived the day.

He stood up to greet Sandrine and Min as they arrived at the table. The pack had dissolved when it was no longer needed, though he still knew where everyone could be reached. He couldn't see himself contacting any of them. Their shared experience, the thing that brought them together in the first place, was much too painful to revisit. He felt it was better to just let the friendships they'd formed fade away in the interest of creating new bonds in the new world.

But Sandrine and Min were different. He needed them in his life to remember how close he'd come to losing everything, to dying in the office of an evil man. He kissed Sandrine on the cheeks, then did the same for Min. The girl was absolutely radiant. She looked older than her years now, after everything she'd been through, but she wore the weight well. Her hair had grown back curlier and darker, and on this day she wore it in a braid over her right shoulder. She squeezed Simon's hand, then sat and took Sandrine's hand under the table.

"The man with the bum leg is the first to arrive. You should all be ashamed of yourselves."

Sandrine shrugged. "Some of us took the time to look beautiful, Monsieur Renaudin."

"A task of ten seconds for lovely ladies like yourselves."

Sandrine laughed and looked out over the street. "Where is your handsome man?"

"He wanted to get a newspaper. Now that it's not full of horrifying stories, he doesn't mind reading it over breakfast."

"Well, hopefully I can convince you both to stick around for a few days. Min and I have been decorating the house. Well, I've been working on the house. Min has taken over the garden. You absolutely have to see the flowers she's planted. I never thought I would want to live with so much color. And the crabapple trees! What an atrocious name for such a wonderful and beautiful thing. She planted one by our back door..."

Simon chuckled as Sandrine rambled on. Sometime after the war, after her recuperation, she'd found her voice. A collapsed lung at the camp nearly took her words from her. Now she was determined to never take the gift for granted again. Simon watched Min listen to Sandrine and saw the adoration in her eyes. In one of her more poetic moods, Sandrine had told him, "I went into Hell and found an angel in the ruins."

Simon felt the same about his own angel. He looked away from Min and saw Kenneth round the corner. His lover was dressed like a professor, his hair grown a bit long on top so he could cover the scar left by his head wound. He looked dashing and urbane, and Simon pushed back his chair. Sandrine stopped talking midsentence and smiled when she saw what had captured his attention. She grinned and settled back in her chair.

Kenneth was reading the paper as he walked. He looked up when Simon clambered over the chain separating the restaurant's dining area from the street. They smiled at one another and Kenneth tucked the paper under his arm to hold Simon's gaze as they closed the distance between them.

During the war, Simon refused to think about the person he would be in peacetime. It seemed too unbelievable to even contemplate such a world. Now that he found himself in a world without war, now that he didn't have to fight and hide every minute of the day, he realized he didn't know anything about himself. The war and the resistance was all-consuming. Here he was, thirty years old and only just trying to figure himself out. Fortunately he had a good partner.

He smiled as he embraced Kenneth on a street too crowded for anyone to pay attention to them. Like Sandrine, he had been through Hell and he'd managed to find his own angel. Together they would try to find some sort of Heaven in the aftermath.

About the Author

Geonn Cannon lives in Oklahoma. He is the author of several novels, including the Riley Parra series which is currently being produced as a webseries for Tello Films, and an official Stargate SG-1 tie-in novel. Information about his other novels and an archive of free stories can be found online at geonncannon.com.